The Sweet Spot

A SWEET ROMANTIC COMEDY

ANNE KEMP

Contents

For my Family

CHAPTER 1

Ari

"Your hand is stuck where?"

This is the perfect example of the danger when living in a small town, when calling 9-1-1 means you'll end up part of the local gossip. Especially when you've given the emergency services operator a comedy gold nugget the size of the Blarney stone.

Taking a deep breath, I repeat myself slowly so Connie can hear every word. "In the toilet, Connie. My hand is stuck in the toilet."

I hear muffled laughter on my end of the phone, telling me Connie's not alone.

"Am I on speaker, Connie?"

"Well..." There's a clamor as she grabs the phone, hits what I imagine is a giant button to turn off the speakerphone as she puts the receiver back to her ear.

"Sorry, Ari, but we have a weekly pool in the office for the weirdest emergency calls. I should be thanking you, 'cause I think I won for the week."

I can tell she's chewing on her laughter still. I hope she chokes on it.

1

I stare at my bathroom wall wondering what I ever did in this lifetime, or any others for that matter, to deserve this very moment. "I guess I should say you're welcome, but I'll follow that up with I want half of any prize money you come into."

My emergency call cohort snorts. "You'll have to pry that fifty bucks outta my cold dead hands."

"It can be arranged." She obviously has forgotten who she is dealing with. "Once I get my hand out of the toilet, of course."

"Your threats don't worry me, sunshine. By the way, loved the write-up you did on the new Italian restaurant in town. Bob and I went the other night and had the best eggplant parm."

I've been writing for the Lake Lorelei News-Post for a few years now, ever since coming back home after college. Not many people get to do what they love, but I managed to find a way.

While Connie's compliments are kind and well-received, I'm literally not in the position for them. I'm wedged between the toilet and my bathtub—like a sugar packet shoved under a table that won't balance—and my knees are starting to cramp. I think my hand is falling asleep. What I really need right now is for Connie to focus on the task at hand—Operation Get My Hand Outta The Toilet. We can talk about the paper later.

"I am so glad you liked it. Hey, Connie, can you tell me when someone might be here to get me out?"

"Oops, okay. Sorry about that. Tell me again how it happened?"

"I was putting on a bracelet in the bathroom and it slipped out of my hands and into the toilet. I could see it just inside where the pipe disappears. So, seeing as it was clean water, I went in after it thinking I could grab it, but somehow my watch got caught on something, and the rest is history. I can't get my hand out now so I called you."

"Are you sure the water is clean?"

I can hear her start snickering again while my all-too-full to-do list cries my name from my living room. "Connie, I have so much on my plate. Please tell me if someone's coming?"

Connie heaves a heavy sigh, breathing out a whoosh into my ear. "Yes, they are. I'm putting out a call now. The guys are at a car accident near the highway so they may not be there for a while."

Great. "What does 'for a while' mean?"

"Assuming you're not in a life-threatening situation?" Connie chortles.

I look around the bathroom. Unless my lotion wants to take me hostage, I'm not in danger. "No, I'm not."

"Good. Then they'll be by after they're clear of that accident. I'll send Truck 41 over to assess the situation, and if anything else pops up, you can call back."

She deserves an award. Those last few words almost don't make it out because I'll be darned if Connie isn't dissolving into snorts and fits of laughter again.

"Thanks, Connie. Front door is open, so tell them they can come in." I start to disconnect the call, but I stop, remembering one more thing. "Oh, and Connie?"

"Yes, dear?"

"Bless your heart," I sing out as I hang up, knowing the use of those three words will have Connie wondering my true meaning for at least an hour. You see, in the South, "bless your heart" has multiple meanings; you just need to slot it in where you see it fits best. I sure knew what I meant, and that's all that matters.

Looking around my tiny tiled cell, I have to trust someone is coming to help. I just pray my brother isn't working on the fire engine today.

I look at my hand where it has merged as one with the toilet. I still can't believe I've managed to do this to myself.

3

Typical Monday morning, right? Only it isn't, and I've got a case of the Monday blues like nobody's business.

It started when I got up for my Monday morning team meeting, which we do for the newspaper over video conference each week. Only this week we were given the news that the physical office for the printed edition will be closing soon and the paper will be going digital only. Our editor-in-chief and owner of the paper, Morris Johnson, gave us the news with a heavy heart, and I was still digesting it.

It wasn't in the cards for me to look for a new job this year. I've just hit my sweet spot with work; I have a column in the paper that I love and it's kicked off a social media influencing side job that I never expected—I'm @alltheyummyfoodies with a following of 65 thousand that's growing daily, plus I get to meet and interview interesting foodies, chefs, and restaurateurs from all over on a weekly basis. Now, I'm nervous and, frankly, really scared all of that could go away.

Looking at the position I'm in now, though, maybe I'm getting what I deserve. It's a theory I don't really want to spend time with, so lucky for me my phone starts ringing.

"Hey, Ari! You free for a quick chat?"

Maisey Montgomery is one of my most favorite people in all of Lake Lorelei. A few years ago, after her mother passed, she took over as the owner of the Red Bird Cafe which was her mama's pride and joy. She's made a name for herself around the area for being a savvy businesswoman who has some serious baking skills—whether she's baking cakes or whipping up pies, you'd swear they were all heaven sent.

"You've caught me at the best and worst time for a chat." I quickly fill her in on my predicament, and Maisey doesn't disappoint.

"Your hand is stuck in your toilet?" She's howling with laughter. Actually howling.

I give her a minute before interrupting. "Are you done now?"

"Oh yeah, for the time being." Maisey chuckles. "I guess you're a hostage audience for me at the moment, so I'll take advantage of that."

"As long as you don't tell anyone—although, Connie knows, which means..."

"...everyone knows by now. Oof. Well, you used to say you wanted to be the talk of the town. Beggars can't be choosers."

Maisey needs to stop talking. "Shush, woman. Whatcha need?"

"Well, I have gone and done something crazy. I wanted to expand the Red Bird, but decided before I do that why not test the waters and see if there's room for expansion, make sure that other people out there love the Red Bird like I do, like the folks here in Lake Lorelei do."

And Lake Lorelei does love the food from the Red Bird. "That is great news! When my hand's free, I'll give you a fist bump of celebration."

"After you've disinfected it. Anyway, I invested in a food truck, and it's finally ready to be unveiled in a few days' time."

"This is more than amazing, Maisey, this is fabulous! A food truck is going to be so popular at all of the outdoor festivals and events in the area."

"That's exactly what I'm banking on. I've been working with Freya to plan a soft launch. She's managed to pull some strings and get an interview with a local television station in Charlotte. They want to feature the food truck, and we thought it would be great to have it operating at the same time as the interview."

I know her niece Freya, and I also know she is a shrewd and sharp social media strategist. "Smart move. Sounds like Freya's on top of things."

"She really is." I can hear the pride swelling in her voice

5

across the line. "She's gone so far as to plan an event so that The Sweet Spot—that's what I'm calling it—will be at the city park for a day. We'll have the food truck pumping, the interview will be live, and I want to have a local influencer there who can help hype folks up. "

I move my body, changing position to keep my shoulder from locking. Is the fire department even coming, or was Connie screwing with me?

"Maisey, this is epic. Congrats to you. How about if I come by later, you know, once my arm isn't attached to my toilet, and I can interview you for the last print edition for the paper? We'll make sure to drive traffic your way for the final edition."

"Oh, that's right. I heard. Morris stopped by after the meeting with everyone on the paper. Are you going to be okay?"

"Sure. I'm like a cockroach, I'm resilient."

"I really hope that's not your spirit animal. Look, I appreciate the offer for the paper and the write-up, and I'll take it, yes please, but I was calling because I wanted to hire you."

"Hire me?"

"I want you to be the official ambassador and social media influencer for The Sweet Spot, if you're willing?"

I was on the floor, floored. "Are you serious?"

"One hundred fifty million percent. Freya and I agree you'd be perfect, but there's a catch."

"Always is. Hit me."

"When Freya lined this up, we thought we'd both be able to go. However, the television station called yesterday to set the date for the interview. It's happening in three days."

"Three days?"

"Yep. It was supposed to be in two weeks' time, but they had a slot open up and can fit us in sooner. Thing is, Freya's out of town until next week and I'm needed this week at the restaurant for some private events we're catering."

My stomach lurches. "You know, I'm thrilled to do it, Maisey. I want to do it, but the timing is impeccable. If you need me to drive to Charlotte, I won't be able to. My car went into the shop a few days ago."

"That's fine. I was going to ask if you'd ride along in the food truck, so you can post the whole time. You see, there's a cool twist to this...the food truck is an old RV that has been quite lovingly refurbished—it's made entirely from recycled materials."

"Great angle."

"That's not all. I wanted this to also be a project for the community, so I'm going to pick a local charity each month that ten percent of our proceeds will be donated to. I want this to be adding more good to the world, you know?"

If I could sit up taller, I would. A part of me flickered with jealousy, hearing Maisey's idea. It was noble and inspiring. I wish I'd had it.

"That sounds amazing, Maisey. I'd love to represent the Red Bird, do the interview, and I'm happy to post, post, post away all day for you!"

"Thank you, Ari." I hear what sounds like a sigh of relief. "Thank you so much. Send me your rates, we've got you covered no matter what."

I look at my hand in its ceramic prison. "Tell you what, as soon as I'm free I'll come by and we'll work out the details."

"Sounds fabulous," Maisey exclaims before asking me to hold for a moment while she answers her other line.

They say timing is everything, and wow. Truth. I've been under financial stress lately— thank you, school loans—and having my car go into the shop right as I find out my job is on the line hasn't done me any favors in the confidence department. I don't want to get too excited, but I swear I already feel my worries beginning to slide off my back.

When Maisey clicks back over, I remember we have one more item of business we need to figure out. "I usually hire a photographer to work with me for campaigns like yours. Do you have the budget for this? I can find someone, but I'll warn you, it is last minute. Fees could be a bit higher than usual, but I'll see what I can do."

"Actually, I've already hired someone. He'll be making the donuts and taking some photos, too. In fact you probably remember him. Carter Snowden is going with you."

I'm sorry, did I hear her right?

"I think the line broke up. Did you say Carter Snowden?"

"I did," she responds. "Weren't you two on the high school newspaper together? You know him, right?"

Oh, I know him alright. Carter Snowden. My brother's best friend and the unknowing object of my affections for years.

I grew up following him and my brother, Reid, around. All the time. Everywhere. If they were hanging out and playing pool in our basement, I was there to fetch them cold drinks and maybe get the chance to play, too. If our family took a summer vacation, Reid always brought Carter with him. I like to think I started writing for the school paper because I wanted to, but a part of me has to admit that I signed up because Carter was the staff photographer.

And then there's that time he kissed me in the darkroom, and promptly asked me to forget about it the next day.

Great.

"Of course, I know Carter, but I don't think he's the right fit for this job." How can I tiptoe around this without sounding absolutely crazy? "Maybe I can see if one of my connections in Charlotte is free. I'm sure I can talk them into a special rate for you."

"No can do. Carter's giving me a great deal on his services to do this. He's also going to manage The Sweet Spot for me part time for its first year. This way I can concentrate on both the restaurant and the food truck without having to be out with the truck all the time. I can't pass up working with someone who's a trained chef, can I?"

"I guess you can't." Now that she's said it, something dings in the recess of my mind and I can hear Reid telling us one night at dinner about Carter going to school to be a chef. Who would of thought? "Do you know where he went to school?"

"He trained out in Los Angeles, then went to France for a year to learn patisserie. How cool is that?"

"Next thing you're going to tell me is that he's a super-hero, but I'll settle for a good photographer. He'd better get my shots right."

"You'll have plenty of time to discuss it because he's driving the truck to Charlotte."

Opening my mouth to lay a heavier case, I'm interrupted by the banging at my front door.

"Maisey, I gotta go. I think my rescuers are here. I'll talk to you later."

I can hear Maisey starting to protest, saying something more about Carter as I hang up, but I just can't right now. I can't hear about the guy who broke my heart in the darkroom that day, the one who inserted himself into so many aspects of my world that I couldn't get away from the ghost of him. Ever.

And the last thing I need for my brother's best friend to know is that for a time, I didn't want to get away from him... but that time has passed.

The banging starts again, more furious this time. "Lake Lorelei Fire Department, call out! Ari, are you in there?"

"Yes! Come on in, I'm in the bathroom," I yell out,

explaining myself, but I'm pretty sure Connie would have set the scene for them by now.

I hear the thumping of boots and shuffling of feet as Lake Lorelei's finest make their way toward me. I manage to turn my body and angle myself so I'm facing the door, greeting the first person who crosses the threshold to my delighted "you're here!!" face.

I just didn't expect that person to be the man of the hour.

Carter Snowden.

CHAPTER 2

Carter

I don't think anyone would believe me if I told them I had thought—no, daydreamed? Fantasized?—about running into Ari Shannon for the last few years. Of course, that daydream never included a toilet, but still. I'm serious when I say I used to see her around almost every corner from Los Angeles to Paris. For me, and because of our circumstances, she's always been the one that got away. She was untouchable. She is untouchable. She's the little sister of my oldest and best friend.

Now, here she is in front of me for the first time in years. Her blonde hair swept back into a ponytail, a pair of cutoff jean shorts hugging every curve like a race car going around turn three on the Daytona track, and her hand is...stuck in a toilet.

"Wow," is the only word that squeaks out when I walk into her bathroom. I watch as she turns, like, fifty shades of red.

"Well. It's nice to see you, too, Carter. Been a while." She sighs. "Reid didn't mention you were back in town."

"Came in a few days ago and started at the fire department part time today."

"That's great. I'd like to welcome you back, but"—she tilts her head in the direction of the porcelain god next to her —"I'm a little busy. Maybe I could get some help here?"

"Wow." Chief Jack McCoy's voice bellows in my ear, having walked up behind me to assess the situation. "This is a good one. Believe it or not, I've seen this before."

Insert loud, audible sigh here from Ari, but I think there's laughter in her voice, too. "Of course you have. Can you maneuver me out of here in one piece?"

Jack kneels down beside her to inspect the situation closer. "The only way to get you out is to take the toilet off the wall, then get you—and the commode—outside. We'll break it open out on the lawn."

Her eyes shuttering closed, Ari breaths out a sigh so deep her shoulders rise and fall.

"That's fine, do what you need to do, please. But, can I ask that we not have any other residents of Lake Lorelei find out about this situation?"

"We'll do what we can, but you know Connie." The chief chuckles as he pats my shoulder. "Carter, let's get it off the wall, then we'll have the guys help us get it outside."

I look down at Ari, who still rocks the brightest shade of red across her cheeks I've ever seen...and I know her shades, trust me. Spending as much time as I did with her family over the years, I got to know all of the Shannons really well. I kneel down next to her, loosening the bolts where the toilet attaches to the floor, having to press into her to get close enough to do my job. When I angle my head to get a better perspective, I'm surprised to find my lips so close to her cheek, but then again the poor woman can't move.

"Sorry, Ari. This is no way to say hello after not seeing

each other for ages. I'll get these loose and we'll get you out of here."

She smiles before turning her head so our faces aren't so close together. "Thank you."

Steam pours off her body, and it's not a good heat. It's the kind of irritated steam that only a Southern woman can emit when backed into a corner. Considering I'm here to help her, and knowing her like I do, she's probably steaming with mortification.

"Well, well, well. My little sister is caught with her hand in the porcelain cookie jar."

Ari's head snaps toward the door as she realizes her brother, Reid, is on the call with us and now standing in her house.

"You could have warned me," she growls through gritted teeth, cutting her eyes in my direction.

"Hey." I incline my head toward the commode. "Don't get mad at me. I'm still getting over the shock of seeing you like this, so I didn't think to warn you that your big brother was here, too."

In true big bro fashion, Reid pulls out his phone and starts snapping pictures of the scene. "Mom and Dad are gonna love this. I'll get it up on Facebook before the toilet's off the wall."

"Shut up, Reid!" Ari's voice is steady and her order is crystal clear. Grabbing a roll of toilet paper she chucks it over my head, smacking the side of Reid's face. Now, this is a side of these two I'm used to. "You're not helping things. Do your job, please, and get me outta here."

Behind Reid, Jack's face appears again. "Bolts off now, Snowden?"

I stand up, giving him a mock salute. "Yes, sir, it's clear to go."

"Good work." He taps Reid's shoulder. "You, take

Snowden and go wait for us in the yard. Dub and I will bring her out, and you two be ready with the sledgehammer."

"The sledgehammer?" Ari chokes.

Leaving the room, I follow Reid back outside and join him on the lawn to wait. This dude has always been a clown and he's not going to give up the title just because we're on a call. He's cracking himself up as he sends the photos he took to his parents. There are probably other family members on that text and a select group of friends, too. These two could be vicious, but in the best way that siblings know how to be—it's always both entertained and terrified me.

"This is awesome." He chuckles, staring at the phone in his hand, flipping through the photos. "Ohhh, be still my heart. I'm going to have mileage out of this for years."

"Dude, think about what you're doing." I shake my head, slugging him in the arm. "That's your sister, Shannon."

Didn't matter, my words only make him laugh harder. "I know. I know. And I can't stop laughing."

I don't want to laugh, but yeah...I'm chewing on my lips now to keep a smile from eating my own face. Ari Shannon always seemed to have it all figured out, while there I was on the side not sure if my shoe laces were still tied. All I ever wanted when we were younger was to get her attention, and believe you me...I tried.

"Head's up, guys!"

Reid and I both spin around. Jack is with Dub, who is also a firefighter as well as Lake Lorelei's local mechanic, and they're walking out slow enough so Ari can keep up, but fast enough so they don't drop the toilet. I take the opportunity to jog over to the engine and grab the sledgehammer from a compartment on the side of the truck. I get back just as they're setting it down. Jack points to a spot on the side, tapping it slowly with his fingertip.

"The porcelain at this point is a bit weaker. If you tap it gently a few times with the sledgehammer, it'll break open and we'll be able to slide her hand out." He turns and smiles at Ari. "All you need to do is cover your face. It won't hurt; it's just going to be loud."

The whole ordeal is over in a matter of seconds. As soon as her hand is free, Ari hops up and takes off running back inside, coming back out a minute later.

"Disinfected." She holds her hand in the air, showing it to all of us. "Did you find my bracelet?"

Jack holds up his hand. "Got it."

"Thanks." Ari's in front of him in a flash, hand out, and palm side up. As Jack drops the bracelet into the safety of her clutch, relief washes across her face. "I'm going to clean this baby off. I'll never put on jewelry in the bathroom again, I can tell you that."

I look at the bracelet in her hand, trying to get a glimpse of it. "Must be a special bracelet for you to go through all of this to get it back?"

"It is." Tucking the bracelet into her front hip pocket, she turns away from me and calls out to her brother. "If I find out you sent pictures to anyone on our family text thread, you know I'm going to fight you."

"You know I don't care." Reid shrugs. "I'm bigger."

"Mmhmm." She taps the side of her head. "But I'm smarter. I'll use my mental skills, therefore I'll wipe the floor with you, Reid Shannon. Don't mess with me. These guys have no idea you used to love the Backstreet Boys. Oh, whoops. Now they do."

There's my girl. That's the Ari I remember.

"In fact, your firefighting buddies should know you were their biggest fan in the area. Weren't you president of their fan club? Do you want 'Everybody' to know?"

Wicked. This woman was still wicked and in the best way possible. When we worked together on stories for the high school paper, I was always impressed by her quick wit and epic comebacks. Pretty good for the daughter of the town's pastor and the little sister of the star quarterback.

Reid is not to be outdone. "Of course 'I want it that way.'"

"Please. 'Show me the meaning of being lonely' is your anthem." Feral eyes flash, taunting her brother.

"You were a fan, too, Ari." Reid lobs one at his sis for the score. "Don't deny your crush on Howie D."

"Puh-lease." Ari cackles, rolling her eyes. "Cry me a river. I was Team Timberlake."

Little secret—I'm enjoying this more than anyone knows. It's been a while since I've witnessed these two in all of their sibling glory. Also, I, too, was Team Timberlake.

"Oh yeah? Bye, bye, bye." Being the big bro he is, Reid effortlessly spins on his heels before walking off to put the sledgehammer away. This is a mistake on his part, but he'll come to the realization on his own eventually.

Ari narrows her eyes, crosses her arms. "You can't ignore me Reid."

"I have, I can, and I will." He is taunting her, clearly not ignoring anyone. An alarm sounds from his pocket, and we watch as he slides his phone out, takes one look at the screen and cracks up. "Well, Mom and Dad like the picture I sent. In fact, Mom even texted saying 'at least you got her good side'— isn't that sweet?"

"Okay, Reid, let's go." Someone needs to be a voice of reason or we're going to have War of the Shannons on our hands. I look at Ari. "It was good to see you today, although from what Maisey tells me it looks like we'll be working together again?"

She nods super slowly. Am I sensing some hesitation here?

"So I'm told. I'm going to see Maisey later today for more info but, yes. She told me we were going to be working together to help get The Sweet Spot going with its first marketing campaign."

"Snowden, you coming?" Jack's rallied the guys back into the engine. When I look over, I find him standing at the door to the cab about to hop in.

"Coming." I turn back to Ari. "We have plenty of time to catch up since we'll be together for a few days."

"Yeah, guess so. Wait, what do you mean a few days?"

"The press junket in Charlotte. Didn't Maisey tell you?"

"We've not fully discussed everything. She only asked if I'd be the official influencer and work the event Freya's organizing." Her features cloud over. At least those red cheeks have toned down. "What have I agreed to, Carter?"

"Maisey told me to block out my calendar for two days. She was waiting for the itinerary from Freya, but it sounds like we have to have the food truck operational, and with food ready, before the 10 a.m. broadcast."

"We're about two hours away from Charlotte. Won't we just leave in the morning?"

"Uh, no." I glance back to the truck and see Jack tapping his watch. "She's going to book us rooms for one night at a hotel near the park there, where we're doing the TV interview."

"What?" Ari's face pales—actual Casper the Friendly Ghost white. "Maisey didn't mention it was an overnight thing."

"Oh." I'm actually twitching now, aware that my boss is holding the fire engine for me to get back into and join my comrades. Crap, it's my first day on the job and I'm already the cog that's holding up the motion of the wheel. "Look, I gotta go. I'll see you soon?"

I jump into the cab and we take off, leaving Ari behind,

staring at the sky. I'd love to know what's going on in that head of hers, but it'll have to wait. We'll be together, side-by-side, no one else with us for a couple of days, so I'll have plenty of time to become fluent in all things Ari Shannon all over again.

Well...fingers crossed.

CHAPTER 3

Ari

I've never been more grateful to be alone in my house. I decided at some point that my love language is more solo and less "yolo," mostly because I simply love to be left alone. I respond best to giant blocks of time by myself, where I recoup my energy and hit refresh on the web browser in my mind. Only my mind is saying "Carter Snowden" on repeat, and dang, that's not helping.

I don't want to think about him right now. I spent plenty of time during my formative years with Carter on the brain. Sounds like an illness, which I guess it was. Lovesickness. Yep, I was one lovesick little sister.

All these years later, when I think about that kiss in the darkroom, I still get shivers up and down my spine. I'm not going to lie, it was a bit awkward and oh my goodness was I nervous as I hadn't kissed anyone before. It was just me and Carter after school; we'd stayed late to finish putting the latest edition of the school paper to bed, and I went into the darkroom with him to pick out our lead images for the front page.

I remember every moment like it happened yesterday. We shared a laugh, our hands touched. It was the first time I had ever felt a jolt hit me in my stomach like a punch, a punch with the sweetest reward on the other side. Instinctively, I had threaded my fingers through his, and we both stood in silence, in the eerie darkness, staring at our intertwined hands. My heart pounded in my chest—I thought for sure he could hear it, but if he did he didn't say anything. In fact, we didn't say much to one another at all.

I am not lying when I say I still feel the weight of his sweet, generous lips on mine. So soft and one hundred percent sensual. I understand the meaning of the word sensual because of his kiss. I floated home that night, excited to see what was ahead for me and Carter and wondering things like, do we tell Reid? Will my parents freak out if Carter comes with us on vacation now? Would people on the paper take us seriously if we were a couple?

In the end, I never needed to worry about any of these problems. My poor little teenage brain. I'd love to hug that girl at some point and tell her don't worry, it'll get better because I'll be darned if what happened next didn't feel like the end of the world...

From my pocket the first chords of "Sorry" by Justin Bieber begin. Don't judge me. I grab my cellphone to answer it, happy it's my mom who's interrupting my trip down memory lane.

"It's been a day and it's not even noon yet," I whine into her ear. "Please tell me you're not calling with bad news."

"You got your hand stuck in the toilet?"

She hasn't even finished her sentence and she's snorting. Yep, my mom snorts. Don't get me wrong, she's cool. Like, ridiculously cool to the point that she and my dad basically adopted any and all of my friends and Reid's friends when we were growing up. Thus how we ended up with Carter being around so much.

"It's true." Dragging my eyes around my living space, I

notice I really need to vacuum now. They were my heroes today, but Lake Lorelei's finest left plenty of dirt. "Have I embarrassed you for the week?"

"Please. You'd have to do better than that. You know Reid got his head stuck in a garage door once, right?"

"No!" I laugh and pace my hallway. "I bet that's a good story."

"I'll tell you about it over lunch. Want to meet me at the Red Bird? We haven't done one of our lunches in a while."

My mom always has the best timing. "Love to. I need to speak with Maisey and was going to go there this afternoon anyway. She's lured me into a job, and guess who I'm going to be working alongside?"

"Uh oh. Do I want to know?"

"It's Carter."

"Ahhh. That's right. Reid said he was coming back into town and might be staying on his couch."

Of course he was.

"He's back and is working today at the fire department with Reid. He'll also be working with me doing a special press event and launch for Maisey. We'll be in Charlotte this week."

"Sounds exciting. I can't wait to hear more."

Is she even listening to me? My mother of all people should understand that even though I am a grown woman now, this is still a horrifying moment for me. Back when the kiss with Carter happened, I wasn't going to tell anyone about it. Especially because of what happened after. In the end, though, I had to tell someone and so I picked the coolest person I knew: my mom, Pat Shannon.

"The last time I really spoke to him was the day he told me we should have never kissed, Mother. If you don't remember, he broke my heart."

"I do remember this. I also remember you discovered Sinead O'Connor's old song 'Nothing Compares 2U' as well and played it on repeat for several days while you worked him out of your system." Her voice trails off and goes quiet. "You did work him out of your system, right?"

"Oh, consider him worked out," I scoff, shoving my hand in my front pocket, making sure that slippery sucker of a bracelet is still there. I feel the cool metal against my fingertips and my insides stop churning and go calm. It's only a charm bracelet—with one charm on it—but it has meaning and I don't want to lose it.

"Good. Sweetie, I'm gonna go and I'll see you in a little bit at the Red Bird."

I hang up only to find a text waiting for me from a number I don't know.

828-555-2512: HI ARI. IF YOU NEED HELP GETTING A NEW TOILET LET ME KNOW. HAPPY TO HELP. :)

This could be one of so many people. I fire a text back.

ME: WHO IS THIS?

828-555-2512: IT'S CARTER. REID GAVE ME YOUR NUMBER.

My tummy dips. No, it drops like a free fall from the Empire State Building. I honestly don't know what to think, so I type a quick reply back.

ME: THANKS. I'VE GOT IT COVERED.

I don't want to sound like a jerk. The man offered to help me buy a new toilet. And we're about to be thrown together for work, so I send another one.

ME: AND THANKS FOR YOUR HELP TODAY CARTER.

That's it from me. I'm leaving it there, but another message comes flying through.

828-555-2512: MY OFFER STANDS, HERE TO HELP. AND IT WAS GREAT SEEING YOU TODAY. IT REALLY HAS BEEN TOO LONG.

My heart flips, and I feel all twisty inside. What does he even mean? Is he being literal, or is there meaning hidden behind his words? Am I reading into things, cause I know I'm good at it. This is why I hate texting; you never really know what the true meaning is that someone's trying to express.

I can't worry about any of this now. I need to grab a shower and go meet my mother. What I really need is to wash that man outta my hair, and outta my thoughts, now.

* * *

"That's a big donut on top of that truck, Maisey. One strong wind..."

"Shush." Maisey holds up her hand, whipping at the air and whipping me away at the same time. "It's a calling card. It says 'The Sweet Spot is here.' Folks will see that donut..."

"...coming for miles."

"I said, shush." She slaps my arm, making contact this time for a skin on skin sting like no other. "They *will* see us coming for miles. Pretty sure we'll stand out with those on top of our truck."

The food truck is cute; it's bright yellow and topped with two giant donuts, one with a pink glaze and the other covered in a faux chocolate.

Standing with her in the back parking lot of the Red Bird and looking at the new food truck, I have to admit Maisey has a point. My mouth waters looking at those large-scale donuts. My tongue dances when I imagine the taste of the coffee I'd wash them down with.

"So, why donuts? Not that there's anything wrong with those, but I would have figured you'd want to showcase your cakes or your pies."

"There's a fun little story there." Maisey grabs my arm and we walk back inside the restaurant, through the kitchen and back to the front of house. "I always say everything happens for a reason, and this is further proof."

I pull out my barstool and settle in next to my mom. "Your reason for this would be?"

"So, I found out through the grapevine there was a truck up for sale in Maryland, right? I called a distant cousin and asked him if he'd go check it out for me, which he did. He also happens to be a mechanic, so he took a look at it to make sure it was going to run and he had other friends make sure it was up to code. Everything looked good, so I gave them a deposit for it. I flew up, and ta-da—giant donuts on my food truck."

"Wasn't your deposit refundable?" I ask.

"No one sent you a picture?" Mom chimes in.

"No and kinda." Maisey rolls her eyes as she refills our sweet tea. "My deposit was non-refundable, and my cousin sent me a picture but somehow managed to cut off the giant ornaments on top of the truck. I gotta say, I understand why my mother didn't want to talk to that side of the family much. Not the brightest bulbs on the Christmas tree."

"Pfft. Well, you gave them a deposit sight unseen." My attempt to be funny falls flat, as evidenced by the amazing scowl crossing Maisey's face. "Sorry, I was aiming for levity."

"Eh." Maisey lifts a shoulder. "Like I said, there's a reason. The truck *is* a donut and coffee truck, but the donuts are going to be based on my pie flavors. So, in the words of Freya, my brand is aligned and we'll be going to the next level."

"Very smart!" I clap my hands together. "You got lemons and you made lemonade. Love it."

"It's the Southern woman's survival skills kicking in." Maisey laughs as she busies herself refilling the sugar caddies on the counter.

"Hope you washed those hands before you ate, Ari."

More joys of living in a small town and sitting at the

counter for lunch at the local cafe. People like to stop by, say hi, and butt into the middle of your business.

"I disinfected and scrubbed 'em, Liz." My grin is tight; I even peel my lips back some and show my teeth trying to look crazy, but Liz doesn't take the hint and sticks around. Liz Donnelly is co-owner of our local bookstore, Read Between the Lines, and leads up the town book club. She's also the queen of leaving her dentures all over town.

Bet she doesn't want me to ask her about her teeth now, does she?

"I've been meaning to ask if you and Pat may want to join us for our community book club one month?" Liz peers over her dark rimmed spectacles which frame her ice blue eyes perfectly. "We're about to vote on next month's pick if you want to jump in."

Beside me my mother bobs her head up and down. "Love to, Liz. I'll stop by the store this week."

Hiding the surprise threatening to wash over my features, I pinch my lips together. My mother is a saint, but she usually steers clear of Liz. Nothing personal, more to do with the town gossip mill. Being the wife of the town's pastor, she likes to fly under the radar as much as possible.

Thankfully her agreeing satiates Liz, who finally trots off to hover over another table. I'm busy watching her when Maisey turns her attention back to us, inclining her head in Liz's general direction.

"Bless her heart. I need to give her a tray and an order pad one day. I swear, that woman does the rounds in this place more than I do on a daily basis." Maisey giggles, leaning closer to us. "She brought her own tea bag with her the other day. Asked me for hot water, steeped her own tea, and sat at the counter for a few hours handing out unsolicited advice."

"We've got plenty of nosy Rosies around here for that now, don't we?" Mom teeters before taking another forkful of chicken salad. "Best recipe ever, Maisey. Another family special?"

"My great Aunt Hattie's recipe. She was an amazing cook."

"Not to change the subject," I butt in completely intending to change the subject, "but I'd love to hear more about the job I'm doing for the Red Bird...or I guess I should say The Sweet Spot, right?"

"You bet." Maisey nods as she puts her elbows on the counter and gets comfortable. "Freya managed to talk a morning television show into doing a live cross from the park where The Sweet Spot will be parked. The episode that day is about specialty North Carolina food trucks. Carter will be making a small selection of donuts for you both to hand out to the folks who show up. It will mostly be the reporters who will be there and maybe a few locals."

"You said reporters, but I thought it was only one TV show that's filming?"

"Ah, this is where it gets tricky." She stands up straight, hands on her hips. "You'll be serving samples starting at seven that morning to any food reviewers, bloggers, and other local reporters who stop by. Freya's asked some of the social media influencers in Charlotte to come, too. You'll have a list of attendees. All of these folks are getting free food, so I want them to be taking pictures, asking questions, and for you and Carter to entertain them and wow them like nobody's business."

"Well." I feel something swipe at my arm. Glancing down, I see Mom's hand flicking the crumbs from my crab cake sandwich off my shirt sleeve. "How did I even get food there?"

"It's in your hair." She points to where my hair's hanging next to my right cheek. "There. It's lump crabmeat, too."

"Can't waste that." I pick it out and roll my eyes in ecstasy as I pop the found food in my mouth, causing my mother to moan in response. Some days I like doing things that are out of my nature just to see her reaction.

Turning back to Maisey, I give her my most charming grin. "Sure you want this gal to be the face of your new baby?"

"Would not want anyone else." She grins, pulling her phone out of her apron pocket. "Let me text Freya and let her know you're in."

"Hang fire, woman, we still need to cover this overnight business." I nudge my mom in her ribs. "She wants us to stay in Charlotte overnight. Me and Carter overnight. Sleeping over in Charlotte."

I fully expect my mother to have my back on this one. Silly as it seems, yes, I am turning into an immature teenager at the very thought of having to face my high school demons...or rather, face the music that is the kiss which was supposed to have never happened.

"You're a big girl, Ari. I'm sure Maisey's not going to force you two to do anything you wouldn't want to do." She shoves another forkful of Aunt Hattie's chicken salad in her mouth and somehow manages to smirk in an all-knowing manner at the same time. "Am I right, Maisey?"

"Yes, ma'am," Maisey sings out with a little bit too much glee. Did she just give me jazz hands?

"Look, Ari." Mom glances my way, talking in between bites. "I didn't want to say anything earlier, but I'm pretty sure that just as you've moved on, so has Carter. It's been years, anyway. You two aren't kids anymore. And your brother was telling me just this morning that he set up a double date that he and Carter are going on this week."

He's going on a date already and he just got into town? My mother's words shake me, but I don't want to let it show. Reminding myself that I'm over him, I wave a hand in the air.

"Like I told you earlier, I worked him out of my system

ages ago." I tap my hand on the counter, twice for good measure. "So. Let's move on. Maisey, you were saying?"

"Gotcha." Grinning, she takes her cue. "I was saying that I'm going to book you two crazy kids a couple of hotel rooms to stay in on Wednesday night. That will give you tomorrow and part of Wednesday morning to get prepped for the campaign before leaving. Is that enough time?"

I pull out my phone and have a seriously disconnected scroll through my to-do list. I shouldn't feel so put out that Carter's going on a date with someone that my ding-dong brother is setting him up with, but I can't help but be a little miffed. Which is dumb, right? It's not like I had thought about him a lot over the years. Maaaaybe once or twice. A month. Fine. A week.

Hating that I feel like this, I push Carter out of my mind and concentrate on the job before me. The newspaper may be shutting its doors on print soon, but I still have a few deadlines to meet before D-Day. "I'll make it all work. Thanks again for asking, Maisey. Your offer came at the right time."

"I'm your unofficial fairy godmother." She tilts her head to the side and looks back and forth between my mom and me. "Tough break on the paper. Do you think there's any chance it could keep going?"

"Morris told me he's retiring and ready to step away," Mom pipes up as she polishes off her lunch. "Unless there's a surprise influx of cash so he can sit back and hire a new editor-in-chief or new investors come along to take over, it's going to be digital-only. Sounds like employees for the digital edition may be sparse because he doesn't think he can pay anyone to keep it going full time."

Her words depress me. How can a town not have a local newspaper? If the Lake Lorelei News is really folding, that means we'll only have people like Connie and Liz to help spread "news"—but that could end up being contentious.

"That is beyond depressing," Maisey sighs, catching my eye. It's like she can hear my thoughts. "What are you going to do, Ari?"

"Haven't had time to dwell on it yet." Okay, it's a little white lie. While Carter may have temporarily taken over residence in my head, his roommate would be my job situation... or rather lack of one. I'm in my denial phase right now, so thinking about this isn't in the cards until later this week. Compartmentalizing is my friend.

But my mother's not a fan of this tactic, darn voice of reason. "Well, you need to dwell on it when you come back this week. When's your car done at the garage?"

"Dylan's going to let me know, but to replace the alternator looks like it will cost around eight hundred, and that's with them giving me a special deal. She talked to her dad; Dub said I can make payments if needed." I hang my head. "It sucks to be worried about this stuff. Adulting is hard."

"Adulting is hard, but you'll get the hang of it. You honestly don't give yourself enough credit for how good you are at being a grown-up." Laughing, my mother stands up and heads to the bathroom. "My treat today. Give Maisey my credit card."

Swiping her purse off the back of her stool, I fish around until I have her wallet in my clutch. Plucking the card from its pocket, I slide it across the counter to Maisey who bypasses the card and grabs my wrist.

"What is *this*?"

She holds my arm aloft, the bracelet in question from my morning's adventure dangling on my wrist. Crap. Out of habit, and probably fear of losing it again, I had put it on before running out to meet Mom—to be fair, I was in a hurry. I had to get to the Red Bird to use the bathroom because I don't have a working toilet at the moment.

29

"It's my bracelet." I'm super nonchalant. Cool, like ice. And igloos.

"Huh." She turns my arm in different directions, inspecting the piece of jewelry. "It's a charm bracelet, right?"

"Sure is."

"And you've had it for a long time?"

Why the third-degree line of questioning? I need to get home and finish my write-up on the new ice cream shop. They have the best banana splits. "Yes, Maisey, I've had it for years. Why?"

"There's something you're not telling me." She points one of her long, skinny fingers at the single charm hanging on the bracelet. "Did you play football in high school, or am I seeing things?"

I glance at the football charm swinging back and forth like a silent traitor giving me away. "You know good and well I did not play football."

She pulls my arm close, so close her eyes cross as she looks over the football charm. "Does that say Snowden?"

Without making eye contact, I nod. Nope. I refuse to look her in the eye right now. I will not. I won't do it.

I did it. I look at Maisey whose face has now given meaning to the phrase "all lit up."

"I knew it." She drops my arm like it's a bad apple and leans across the counter, whispering. "Do you still have feelings for him?"

"What? No." I shake my head so hard I give myself whiplash. Looking at the bracelet, I silently tell myself off for even wearing it today. It had been nothing but trouble since this morning. "Carter was a big part of my life growing up. This"—I hold up my arm—"is a childhood memory that I happen to value. It represents a time in my life before things got too...complicated."

"Mmmhmm." Maisey's lips twitch. "You've got it bad. I bet no one even knows, do they?"

"He's my brother's best friend, Maisey," I snap, but not in a serious way. "Therefore, he's off-limits. He was then, and he is now."

"You're both adults. Who says he's off-limits?"

"Reid."

She rolls her eyes. "And when did he tell you this?"

"When we were in high school. Reid pulled me to the side and told me I was to never date any of his friends."

"Girl, you listened to him?"

"Yes and no." I shriek with laughter, finally breaking. "It was Carter who kissed *me* and then he told me the next day we needed to forget it ever happened. The end. I left for journalism camp a few weeks after that, and when I came home, I made sure to avoid him as much as possible."

"We'll discuss the fact that you went to journalism camp another time. I want to clarify, though, that your moment with this man was like...ten years ago?"

When she puts it like that, I sound reality TV show nuts. "Give or take."

"Ari. You don't think it could be time to move on?" She turns to face me square on as my mom slips back into her seat beside me.

"Is she still talking about Carter?" Swirling on my stool, I'm surprised to catch my mom pulling a face. "Yawn. I'm going to change the subject. You need a new toilet, so I've decided I'll go with you and we'll organize one to be delivered while you're away this week. You can stay with your dad and I for a few nights until it's put in."

If I had a dime for the amount of times today I heard the word toilet used in the same sentence as my name, I swear I'd be rich. Not Bezos rich, but like...able to live comfortably rich.

"Sounds like a plan." I grab my things and stand up ready

31

to go. Mom's already got one foot out the door, headed to start the car.

Hands come down on top of my shoulders from behind. "Freya will email you all the info you need, and I'll leave it to you and Carter to organize when you're leaving. I just ask that you make sure everything goes smoothly, especially that live cross for the morning show."

Spinning around, I give her a mock salute. "You got it. Thank you again for thinking of me. I'll do you proud."

"I have no doubt you both will." She locks me in her sights, still holding on to my shoulders. "Look, I may have said it was time to move on, but only you know how you feel. One thing I was taught by a very wise woman a long time ago is that you don't find love. Love finds you. Stay open, dance with possibility, and have fun, okay?"

Maisey pulls me into a quick hug before pushing me off in the direction where my mother had gone. "Now, go on. Go get yourself a new toilet."

Jogging away from Maisey, I tuck the bracelet inside my sleeve where it's usually hidden and stroke the tiny football with my fingertip.

As anxious as I feel about going away with Carter alone this week, I need to be totally honest with myself.

I couldn't be happier.

CHAPTER 4

Carter

I don't remember ever making a drive from Lake Lorelei to anywhere that felt this electric. Maybe it's one-sided, I don't know. What I do know is that Ari's sitting mere inches from me and I can smell her shampoo. Floral notes, for sure.

Trust me, I feel creepy even thinking about it, but the scent makes me heady.

Since the moment I picked her up, she's shielded herself by hiding behind her phone and "working". As The Sweet Spot's ambassador I know Maisey would have asked her to do some basic posting, but knowing Ari like I do, she'll go way above and beyond. I have a feeling that if it also has the added bonus where she can avoid me, she'll keep her nose buried in her phone all day if she can.

So far she's done some stories for Instagram, even forcing me to be in a few, which is fine. I signed up for it, so I'll go on camera if she wants. I've made sure to pull over a few times and take some pictures as well, showing the truck in various spots along the drive; with the mountains in the background, at a rest stop I had Ari pose like she was serving at the window, and I managed to talk her into climbing on the roof and sitting on the donuts, too. The photos are fun and ones I know Maisey will love using for any ads or marketing campaigns she runs in the future.

Ari has spent the last thirty minutes posting a selection of the photos I've taken and sharing them with her followers, plus posting them on the Red Bird's official pages, too. There's been a flurry of clicking, tapping, posting, and engaging, but now it seems that she's finally taking a break.

Grabbing one of my road trip snacks—Haribo gummy bears, no imposters here, please—I hold the bag out to her.

"Want some?"

I stare at the road in front of me, but I feel her looking at me, contemplating my offer. I wait until her hand is almost inside the bag before snatching it back.

"Did you disinfect your hand first?"

"Et tu, brute?" Ari thrusts her hand in the bag, pulling out an obscene amount of gummy bears. I hear them crying, her grip is that tight. "I can't be the only fun piece of gossip in town these days. It would be a sad state of affairs if so."

Her voice drips with irritation, so I'm going to rain check being playful right now.

"If it makes you feel any better, I'm pretty sure there's other gossip happening."

"Mmm." She turns in her seat again, facing me. "Like the double date you went on with Reid last night?"

I think I snap my neck as I turn to look her in the eyes. "How did you...?"

"Social media is my friend." She holds up her phone. "Reid posted a picture of the four of you out for dinner. You do know that Dylan and Reid aren't a couple, right?"

I don't need to see the picture to know the one she's talking about. Dylan, who's a firefighter as well, was hosting her cousin for a night so she asked if we'd go out with her and show her cousin a good time. I know this, but Ari doesn't.

"Someone needs to tell Dylan and Reid they aren't a couple because they act like it."

"Reid would be lucky if she ever gave him a second look like that." She chuckles. "Dylan's a rock star."

"She's pretty cool and so is her cousin, for that matter." Am I being immature, letting Ari think it had been a date for me? Yes. Do I think I may regret it later? Probably, but I'm going to let it play out. For now. Why? Because I can't tell her that all I thought about at dinner that night was her. I thought about Ari with her hand in the toilet, I thought about Ari with her hand out of the toilet.

I thought about her even as I sat next to her brother at dinner, my best friend who had warned me all those years ago to stay away from his little sister. I thought about driving over to Ari's house after we ate, knocking on her door, and planting a kiss on those full, pink lips of hers. If memory serves, they're soft and sweet, and this time I know I'll never want to stop.

"I bet she is." Ari interrupts my daydream, murmuring under her breath as she closes her phone and tosses it to the floor at her feet. "Anyway, lover boy, we've got time to kill. Let's talk about you. Pastry chef?"

"That would be me. I guess you're wondering how I got into it?"

"Definitely." She grabs her phone again, in one swift motion. "Should we post about it?"

Horrified, I look over and find a wicked smile playing on her lips. "Ha. You got me."

"Good." She cackles. I know that laugh; it's usually reserved for when she's playing a prank. "I guess it's a surprise to me because in all the years I knew you before, you never seemed to be the guy who was in the kitchen."

Oh the irony of the statement. "You never saw me in the kitchen much because I was always at your house. If you had ever come to my place, you would have seen that I was the man when it came to meal prep. I made sure Dad and I had food on the table for all three meals. I even did the grocery shopping."

"Impressive." A low whistle echoes in the cab of the truck. "Had no clue."

"When I graduated, I wasn't good enough for football and I didn't know what I wanted to do, not that we could afford very much. Dad talked me into going to California to stay with relatives. While I was there, I started working part time at a restaurant in Santa Monica called Michael's. The pastry chef was insanely talented and inspiring. She took me under her wing, and I took off from there. Ended up in Paris studying patisserie from her old teacher."

"Not everybody would get the chance to really explore what they want to do. I'm jealous you got to unabashedly pursue a true passion."

"Well, now, hold on. Reid's kept me up-to-date on you, too."

"He has?" Was that genuine surprise I heard?

"Of course he has. He's proud of you, Ari. They all are. You're writing for the paper, reviewing restaurants, it seems like your influencing and freelance work is taking off...at least from what he tells me."

"Huh." I sneak a peek as she crosses her arms, hugging herself close. "I didn't know Reid kept tabs like that."

"He's your big brother. It's his job to be annoying and a pain in the butt, but it's his duty to be proud."

"Well, it'll be fleeting." I hear sadness in her tone.

"Why's that?"

There's an energy shift in the cab as she speaks. "I guess you've heard by now the paper is closing its doors."

Ah. "I did. I'm embarrassed to say I didn't put it together until now. Crud, sorry about that, Ari."

"We'll still be digital, but we're losing the printed edition, which to me is the heart of the paper. It's the heart of the town, really. I mean, can you remember a time that the paper wasn't outside your Dad's front door in the morning?"

"I used to deliver that paper back in the day; it was my first paycheck." I puff up my chest with pride, making her grin. Job done. "Is Morris selling the building, too?"

Ari bobs her head up and down in my peripheral vision. "He's dumping it all. Ready to retire."

"That first floor is one of the sunniest spaces in Lake Lorelei. I could never get over how open and big the second floor was, too. Talk about being in a prime location across the street from the fire department, police station, and courthouse."

"Totally agree," Ari concurs. "It's the end of an era, really, and I'm going to miss it. I think Morris was thinking of turning the downstairs into a cafe or some kind of retail store before he decided to retire. It needed something; it was another space with so much to offer." She sighs. "Hopefully whoever buys it won't do something dumb like tear it down."

I visibly shudder at the thought, which doesn't escape Ari's keen eye. "You cold?"

"No, just thinking. You know that I'm going to be running The Sweet Spot for the first year it's open?"

"Will you be able to juggle it, what with being in the fire department, too?"

"I'm only doing a very part-time role for the fire department. I'm filling in when they need me right now. Your brother wanted me on the roster, and I couldn't say no."

Which is something I was sure she'd understand if she only knew more about me. For someone that I spent a lot of time with when we were younger. I've also managed to keep a

37

lot hidden from her as well. Like the fact that there was a time when my dad couldn't function enough to get food on the table when my mom left us. That's why I know how to cook, and it's also why I ran far away from Lake Lorelei when I was able to go. Coming from a broken home with little support? I didn't want to be that guy, the one who everyone in town felt bad for when they figured out my dirty secret. A secret that only Reid knew. That I was going home to be the adult to my dad who was a dumpster fire at the time.

Reid had witnessed my home life and seen it up close. He'd been there and helped me pick my dad up off the floor when he'd had too many beers during the day and couldn't help himself. I only had to ask Reid once to not tell a soul and he promised me he wouldn't, and to this day he hasn't. I don't even think his parents know the lengths I would go to for my father.

So, yeah, when my best friend asks me to help him, or stay away from his little sister, I'm going to listen. Even if it's one of the hardest things I have to do.

"Reid can be convincing; I've seen it firsthand. He can charm our mother to no end."

"Exactly. And yes, to answer your question, I think I can juggle it all. I have to because I'm toying with the idea of opening my own restaurant—maybe—around here in the next year or so. That's why I'm working with Maisey 'til I can figure out what I want to do."

"Really? Maisey doesn't mind?"

"She's all for helping me get my name out there because she knows my idea is to have an upscale BBQ joint, not a cafe. Fried mac and cheese but with class."

"Oh my. Did you just put mac and cheese into its own class?" If I'm not mistaken, she just choked on a gummy bear in between giggles. "I tell you what, some fried green tomatoes could be done classy, too, you know."

"You know what I mean." My turn to chuckle. "You always did take everything so literally."

"I do it so I can understand, Carter. It's the Virgo in me— we're organized and have to know what's going on. Our brains are analytical."

"Virgo. That means what?"

"It's my astrological sign, goof. My birthday is in September."

"It's the fifteenth, right?" Boy, do I seem eager or what?

"Very good. I see all of the Shannon birthdays you were forced to attend stuck with you."

The Shannons were always great at birthday celebrations, mine included. Birthday dinners were your choice, with a desert also of your choosing, and the night was all about you. Amazing for a kid like me to be a part of, I'll tell you.

"For the record, I was never forced to attend."

"Noted. Your birthday is in March, right?"

"Yup." I nod, impressed with her memory now. "March ninth."

She taps the dashboard three times, telling me she's had an ah-ha moment. Yes. I know her taps, too. "Now this is starting to make sense to me."

"What?"

"Us. You're a Pisces and I'm a Virgo. We're yin and yang."

"We're Carter and Ari."

"No, listen." She laughs as she leans across the cab and play smacks my arm. How dare I relish her touch. "There are astrological signs that are really super compatible, that work well together. Virgos and Pisces are one of these perfect pairings."

"Like when we were on the school paper together?" My approach is meant to be playful, but I miss the mark. As soon as the words tumble out I want to take them back. If she was like me, and judging by the dark cloud suddenly appearing over her head and the scowl crossing her face, I just transported us both back in time to a darkroom long, long ago.

"Something like that." Her tone is deadpan as she grabs her phone and turns her body to face the window. "I should get some more posts up for Maisey."

And just like that, I'm on the other side of the wall. I stare at the road for a time, driving in silence, and am blissfully surprised when I see our exit up ahead. It's been a busy week, and a long day. I'm looking forward to getting a good night's sleep.

About thirty minutes later, I maneuver the food truck, giant donuts and all, into a parking spot. Jumping out from behind the wheel, I stretch my arms overhead and take in the old motel sign. It's one of those old retro ones, you know the kind where you can tell this place has some stories, right? I'm pretty sure the motel owners have seen some good times here. At least the dilapidated building is still standing, but man it has taken a beating.

Ari hops out and walks around to my side of the truck so she can grab her suitcase. It's my time to shine and show her my chivalrous side. I know, I'm starting small, but I've got deep issues to sort out here and layers of this woman to cut through.

We had piled our suitcases on top of some boxes stuffed with accessories, menus, and other swag that Maisey sent with us. Opening the door to the back of the truck, I hadn't expected everything to shift during transit, but it sure did.

As the door opens, both of our suitcases spring out, hitting the pavement beside us. My suitcase is pretty tough and bounces, while Ari's, unfortunately, can't handle the intensity. As soon as it hits the ground, the suitcase flies open and everything she packed—and I do mean EVERYTHING—comes shooting out around us. And on us.

I feel a twack on the top of my head as an errant piece of clothing smacks me. Oh boy. I think her bra is on my head.

"You've got to be kidding me!" Ari shrieks while I stand perfectly still swallowing my laughter. When I turn to look at her, a range of emotion floods her features—there's those shades of red again—as it registers that her bra is hanging on my noggin. Rage, embarrassment, surprise... Yup. She's feeling it all.

She reaches up and swipes her brassiere from my head, the shoulder loop getting hung up on my ear. I'm cringing now, but the assault of red coloring across her face at this moment? Priceless.

I grab the fabric and untangle it from my ear and throw it in the open suitcase while Ari turns on her heel and drops to the ground, scooping up shirts, underwear, toiletries, and shoes, shoving it all back into her luggage.

"I thought we were here for one night?" I hold up a dress that's managed to land at my feet, trying to infuse some humor. "This is fancy. Do you call this your LBD?"

I've thrown out a line, but this fish? She's not biting.

"I like options, Carter," she hisses, snatching it out of my hand and stuffing it along with the other stray items back inside the suitcase. Plunking herself down on top of her bag, she slams her full weight into it and forces it shut again. "Most women do, you know."

"Noted." Sassy. She's so sassy, and I'm here for it. "Women like options."

I incline my head in the direction of the motel's front office. "Want to get our rooms then grab some dinner?" Glancing around, I see at least five different restaurants within walking distance. "We have *options* for our meal, if that suits my lady."

Ari grunts, hauling her suitcase to the sidewalk. I reach out to take it, but she passes it to her other hand. "I can handle it myself, Carter, but thank you. Don't need a repeat performance, do we?"

One thing I now know for certain is that this woman is embedded in my being. The crush I had on her when we were younger is more than alive and well. We're not kids anymore—which the contents of her suitcase have shown me.

Ari's always been this beautiful enigma to me—my best friend's little sister who I always liked teasing. The little sister who had pigtails for the pulling. Now, she's the little sister who I want to sweep off her feet and make her mine.

I walk behind her in silence toward the entrance, both frightened and fascinated by what's to come. Fascinated, because if that moment in the darkroom years ago told me anything, it was that we have chemistry. My job is to win this woman over and get her trust back, cause I'm pretty sure that's the reason she freezes up with me.

Frightened because I made a promise to Reid years ago, but that is one I'm definitely second-guessing now.

CHAPTER 5

Ari

"Y ou only have one room available? This can't be."

The reservation slip in my hands shows two rooms. I hold up the piece of paper to show the woman behind the desk, pointing to the info she needs. "See. One for him and one for me." In an attempt to be helpful, I'm leaning over the front desk trying to see the motel reception-ist's computer screen. Maybe if she lets me look I can help her —but she won't. Glaring at me, she grabs the monitor and swings it away from my prying gaze.

I watch as she pounds the keyboard, her fingers dancing across it in a frenzy. I'm keeping time with her and tapping my fingers on the countertop. As if the last ten minutes of my life hadn't been embarrassing enough, thanks to my inept packing skills, now I'm being told I might have to share a room with Carter?

"I'm sorry. I don't know what happened." Swiping a hand through her rainbow-dyed tresses, she clicks her tongue and scratches her head. As mad as I am, I can't unleash my anger on this woman. She's young, still has braces, and her hair is way too cute for me to yell at her. It's probably her family's motel and she's stuck here on night duty. "I see the reservation is still here, but it's for two people. In one room."

Sensing I'm not going to win this round, and not having any energy in me to push harder, I pivot for Plan B. Both Carter and I need to get some sleep before tomorrow's event. "Okay, fine. Can we have a rollaway bed brought to the room, please?"

My new friend goes back to her computer and taps away. I stride over to the makeshift coffee station and pour myself a small cup. Brewed fresh and smells oh-so-good. I take a long sip as she chats away.

"I think we have...oh, no. I'm wrong. Goodness gracious, you're out of luck tonight aren't you? We don't even have any rollaway beds you can use."

I spit my coffee back into the cup. "Seriously?"

She nods, shrugging her shoulders. "It's a busy week. There's an art fair in town and I think there's a race at the speedway. What can I say, it's summer." She grins at me one last time as she slides the key over and turns away to answer the phone, none the wiser that she's just burst my bubble of sanity.

Thankfully, when I go back to the truck, Carter's in as much shock as I am, but he's quicker to think of a plan.

"I'll just sleep out here tonight."

"You can't do that. I feel bad."

"Good." He wiggles his eyebrows at me, making me laugh even though it's the last thing I want to do right at this moment. "Seriously, I'm happy to stay out here. It's one night, right?"

One very humid September night outside in North Carolina. The air is so crazy thick, I'm having a hard time taking a breath. "It is only one night, but...are you sure?"

He nods again. "Positive. You're going to be the front woman, anyway. I get to hide in the back of the truck or behind the lens. I have to be up really early, too, in order to get the ovens going and have the food prepared for a 7 a.m. start."

As happy as I am that I get to go and close the door to my very own motel room tonight, and sleep safe and snug in bed, I can't help but feel horrible for Carter. He's getting the crap end of this stick tonight. "Do you want to come in and grab a shower at least?"

Carter shakes his head and tosses his overnight bag back inside the food truck. "I'll just grab a pillow and a blanket for now, but I'll take you up on the offer tomorrow before we do the interview."

"Deal." I jog to the room, grab Carter a pillow and blanket, and race back out. I'm so close to being able to close the door and be alone, I can taste it.

As I hand him the pillow, his hand accidentally brushes mine and we both seem to freeze. I'm staring at our hands, willing mine to move, while deep inside me a tiny flip turns over in my stomach. I don't want to look at him. I'm more than aware of his presence, the subtle scent of his cologne hitting my senses as he steps in closer to lift the items from my arms.

Unreal. How is it that this man can cause this kind of current to race through my system? There's a shiver beginning at the tips of my toes, snaking all the way up to the crown of my head. I look up to find Carter standing in front of me and my breath hitches. He's watching me with what I'd describe as interest, that's for sure. But the look in his eye reminds me of that time long ago when I succumbed to the moment and childishly thought he had too.

Awkwardness washes through my system, flushing away the rush. I step back, ready to ignore the look of confusion registering across his face—only things never go the way I want them to.

I don't see that there's a step stool behind me. Why would

it be there? We're in a parking lot. The stool? It usually lives in the food truck, but Carter must have brought it out when he started re-arranging things for the night.

Head over heels, that's the saying, right? I flip backward, literally looking at my feet high above me as they fly into the air. I'm wearing my good Converse, the ones without shoelaces, because who has time to tie their shoes, anyway? At least they're new.

I'm not telling you the best part, though.

In my infinite wisdom, I decided to wear a skirt today. I'm repping The Sweet Spot, so I wanted to look cute. So while I managed to get my bra off Carter's head, he now has a full view of my backside—and my pink-and-white checkered underwear—as my skirt flies up and I fall flat on my back in the middle of the parking lot.

"Ari!"

Good man, he's by my side in record time, kneeling next to me.

"Are you okay?"

"No." I slap my hands over my face, threading my fingers tightly, wanting to cover and hide. Something in my back clicks. Probably a rib. "My ego is mortally wounded and my back hurts like I was hit by a truck."

"I can't help with the ego, but I can help you stand up." His voice has the tone of concern, but I know he's waiting for a cue to laugh. I mean, I would be if I were in his shoes.

"I didn't hit my head, so that's a win, right?" I look up to see Carter's hand stretched out to help me up. I take it, letting him pull me to my feet. Brushing myself off, I'm absolutely delighted to find a Twinkie wrapper stuck in my hair. When did my hair become fly paper for food?

"I'll throw that away." Peeling it off my tresses, I thrust the old wrapper in my pocket not wanting to admit I could seriously tear into a Twinkie right now. Emotional eating is a real thing, and thankfully I spied a vending machine near my room.

Carter's biting his bottom lip now in a good effort to not laugh in my face. Oh, he is so much better than me; I'd be dying with laughter if this had been him. Only it wasn't, and here he is being really super sweet and helping me out. My hero again. Dang it.

* * *

"Carter said he's got his part for tomorrow under control. We prepped most of what he needed, so you won't have to worry about anything he's doing. All you have to do is keep posting your photos, tag in the people Freya wants tagged for social media, and give a good interview when the time comes. Sound good?"

Maisey's dying inside that she's missing the launch of her baby, but I love that she trusts us to get it across the line.

"What could go wrong?" I hear the words and want to slap myself for saying them out loud.

"Bite your tongue and take that back," Maisey huffs. "I'd love to know how they messed up my reservation for you two. And poor Carter's in the truck. What is it, like ninety-five degrees tonight?"

"I think it was eighty last time I checked." Yuck. Sitting on top of the bed in shorts with air conditioning blasting around me, I'm feeling even more guilty. Climbing off the bed, I open the curtain and peer out into the parking lot to check on the truck and Carter. It's dark except for the occasional flicker of a light from inside, probably from his phone or a flashlight.

"I hope he doesn't get sick sleeping in the heat," Maisey clucks, adding to my guilt.

"He volunteered to stay in the truck, you know."

She's right, though. I don't want him to get sick either,

and I hate myself for being comfortable while knowing he's outside and probably miserable.

Maisey and I disconnect but not before I pinky-promise to touch base tomorrow after the event. I no sooner put the phone down before I'm back at the window, looking at the truck. That small truck, with no air conditioning going on this sweltering hot night.

I turn my head toward the heavens and shake a fist. "Fine! I'll go get him!"

When I approach him, he acts like he's doing okay, but I can tell from the copious amounts of sweat seeping through his shirt and the damp on his brow that he's miserable.

It doesn't take long to convince him to come inside.

As soon as he crosses the threshold into the room, he points to the bathroom. "I'm going to hop in the shower now, if that's okay."

"Go for it." I toss him a towel.

While he's in the shower, I call and ask for an extra sheet to be delivered. Luckily Cara, my new BFF also known as the girl who works at the front desk, is still around. She brings me one and, surprisingly, a roll of duct tape.

"Um, well." I hold up the tape, inspecting it. "This is...unexpected?"

"It's for the sheets, so you can tape it to the ceiling." She peers inside the doorway of the room, winking as she points to the bed. "I assumed you two were probably sharing the room now. You may want to set some boundaries."

"I would never have thought of that." I'm standing with my back to the room, nodding and thankful for my cohort's quick thinking. "Very smart. Thank you."

Cara's nodding when her line of sight suddenly shifts over my shoulder, looking beyond me into the room, and her eyes widen. Turning, I see what's gotten her attention.

Carter had emerged from the bathroom as we talked and is

now standing in the middle of the room, dripping wet with a towel very loosely wrapped around his waist. My stomach dips, Cara's breath catches behind me. I fight the urge to put my hands over her eyes.

Good thing he's managed to wrap the towel just below that perfect V-shape of his abs. If his intention was to drag our eyes there, it worked.

I snap out of my haze when Carter coughs. He's looking back and forth between Cara and me; she's holding the sheet, I'm holding the duct tape.

"Should I ask y'all what's going on?"

"I'll be leaving now," Cara murmurs as she backs away, pushing the sheet into my hands. In the corridor, she mouths "good luck" and gives me a thumbs-up, then she trots off, leaving me with a half-naked man standing in front of me.

"It's for us." Turning slowly after closing the door, I find a pair of wide eyes waiting for me to explain. "I'm going to make a wall for us. With the sheet."

"Ah." He pivots and goes back into the bathroom, taking his overnight bag with him. I hope he's planning to put some clothes on now. I don't think my heart can handle it. The darkroom as teens is one thing, but a motel room as adults—with that body?—is dangerous. "Boundaries. I get it. We can put a wall of pillows between us, too, if you want."

"No, a sheet is fine." Chewing on the side of my cheek so I don't giggle, I double-check myself in the mirror. The way things have been going lately I want to make sure all of my clothes are on the right way and that I don't have anything stuck in my teeth. "I trust you won't roll onto my side; I just want to feel like we have some space."

"Whatever you need." The door opens to the bathroom, releasing a cloud of steam into the room.

We stand still for a few moments looking at each other. I don't think I'll ever be able to erase the memory of his defined

49

and sculpted body, but I know I don't ever want to. I feel like if I wanted, like really, really wanted, I could get a darkroom do-over with Carter right now. As much as I'd like to, I can't ignore that I still feel a sting from his desire to erase the moment years ago.

If I wasn't good enough for him then, why would I be now?

I break our gaze and hop up onto the bed. In a matter of minutes, I have our sheet-wall put up and I climb under the covers on my side. Carter rustles around in the bathroom, brushing his teeth and doing who-knows-what while I lie here. Sheets pulled up under my chin—tight—while staring at the ceiling wondering how we got here.

As kids, it was nothing to pile together in a bed. This would happen sometimes, but we were little. And even though it's been years since I last saw Carter, he's been a part of my life for longer. I find myself walking through the dangerous neighborhood that is my mind, wondering if I have truly packed away my feelings for him, then why is it I'm feeling so weird now?

"Bombs away!" The bed shakes as Carter throws himself onto his side. The curtain between us pulls back, and he peeks around it. Keeping his face covered except for his eyes. "Boo."

"Stop it." I swat him, laughing.

He drops the curtain, but pulls it back suddenly and points to my wrist. "Is that the bracelet we fished out for you the other day?"

I shove my hand under the sheet. "It is. Should probably lock it away; I feel like it's a bad luck charm these days."

"I'll be glad to take it off your wrist if that's what's causing your trouble." Grinning, he lets the sheet drop so we're separated again and turns out his light, surrounding us in darkness. "We can throw it in the lake when we go home."

I shudder, physically reacting to the suggestion. Touching

the bracelet with my other hand, I hold the charm between my fingers, stroking it. Twenty bucks says he doesn't remember giving this to me.

"So." Carter clears his throat. "This isn't weird at all, right?"

I let go of a raucous laugh, and it feels good, and Carter cracks up on the other side of our fabric divider. "I'm glad you said it. It's sooo weird."

"It's nice to be back." He sighs. I feel movement as he rolls over. "I'm finding there's a lot about Lake Lorelei I missed."

"Things have changed while you were gone, but luckily most of it is the same." I roll my eyes hearing myself speak. What a dork. Subject change. "Well, except for the paper. I'm going to miss my job."

"You're a great writer, Ari. I've seen the columns you've written here and there, over the years. Maybe you can do a similar role at another paper? Or do more with your influencing role?"

My stomach sinks at the suggestions, however well-meaning. "I could, but I don't know." I roll over on my side so I'm facing the sheet, imagining he's right there on the other side, mimicking my position like a mirror image. "Please, don't get me wrong. I love writing about food and restaurants, and I've enjoyed meeting and interviewing so many chefs over the years. And the social media gigs have been cool, but...I don't know. It feels empty. I feel empty. Talking to Maisey about the charity contribution she's doing with The Sweet Spot got me thinking I need something more. As cheesy as it sounds, I want to make a difference. Go home at the end of the day really proud of the mark I'm leaving on this world."

"You'd get that with social media, wouldn't you?" he asks.

"Not really. Not like I could with something else. I don't know, a bigger platform maybe? My own TV channel?" I know, I'm reaching for the stars.

"Go big or go home." Carter chuckles. "What does your family say?"

I snort. "Not much. Mom tells me I'll figure it out. Dad says listen to your mom."

"No input from Reid?"

"No." I let out a sigh, closing my eyes. "Believe it or not, it's not so easy being the little sister of Reid Shannon: fire-fighter, star quarterback, and currently known as the most eligible bachelor in town. Not when you're the sibling who's losing her job, struggles to pay her bills, and gets her hand stuck in her own toilet."

"Certainly not your finest hour." Carter says with a snicker. "But don't let it define you."

When did his voice take on this velvety-rich texture? I swear, I could listen to this man talk all night.

"I hear your words, and I'm going to take them on board."

"Good. Now don't throw them off the boat." He stifles a yawn. "Thanks for coming out to get me. It was really hot in the truck."

"If it makes you feel any better, I was in here feeling guilty the whole time you were out there." My turn to snicker. "Being guilt-ridden is another trait for a Virgo. Just FYI in case you're interested."

"What about for a Pisces?"

"Yep, same except your guilt comes out at night when you're trying to sleep. A lot of Pisces have insomnia. Why? Having trouble sleeping lately?"

"I've had my share of guilt over the years," Carter whispers, moving in his spot again and causing the bed to shake. "Come to think of it, I had bouts of insomnia when I was in high school."

If this man ever felt guilt to the point he had insomnia when we were younger, he covered it well. "Do you know why that was?"

He's quiet. Opening my eyes, I stare at the sheet and imagine he's lying there doing the same. I take my hand and gently slide it so it's next to the sheet, this eclectic current beginning to fizz inside of me again.

"I have my suspicions," he whispers.

Now I'm curious. "Feel like sharing?"

"Well." He clears his throat, keeping his voice low. "There was this girl, and I think I had a crush on her. But I screwed up, you see."

Even though I feel like I know where this is headed, I bite. "What happened?"

"Looking back, I think I was nervous. This girl seemed unapproachable even though I knew her well." He pauses, his voice hushed. "Do you remember that time in the darkroom?"

Does a dog bark? "I do."

We're both quiet. I feel safe talking about this in the dark, but it also feels unknown.

"I messed up," he whispers, his voice thick like melted caramel. "We were young and your brother didn't want me to go near you."

"You know what, Carter, you don't need to explain." Memory lane needs a roadblock for now. I've been riding an emotional roller coaster for a few days, and honestly, I think we both need sleep. "As much as it hurt, you were right. We crossed a line at the time. You just saw it first."

I know I'm saying these things, but how do I tell him that I'm lying here having *all* the feelings and I can't sort them out because his presence is so big to me that I can't think?

"I hate that I hurt you." He's quiet for a second before he continues. "I'm sorry that I did. You have to understand that my loyalty was to your brother. He was and is my best friend, Ari. At that time, he knew me better than I knew myself."

Something tugs on my heart—but I need to stop this

ANNE KEMP

conversation for now. I glance at the alarm clock beside the bed. "It's almost midnight. I should get some sleep."

"Yeah, me, too," he agrees. "Nite."

"Good night." I roll over, putting my back to the sheet, and to Carter, and close my eyes. Hearing the rhythm of his breathing, it's a reminder that the sexiest and most interesting man to walk (back) into my life in years is lying only mere inches away from me right now.

Tomorrow's a big day with The Sweet Spot being the star, but I have a feeling that tonight in my dreams, someone else may be taking center stage.

CHAPTER 6

Carter

I'm whipped and worn out, but grateful for how busy the morning's been. My eyes are blurry from my lack of sleep last night. I tossed and turned most of the night, while Ari snored as loud as a buzz saw, and I didn't bring ear plugs with me. But it wasn't the noise that kept me up.

How was I to sleep when Ari lay just a few inches away from me with only a sheet to separate us, confusing my male mind?

"Carter, can you take a pic of us?"

Ari's voice pulls me out of my haze. I look out the window of the food truck to where she stands on the grass, flanked on either side by food influencers Freya had invited for the sampling. I have to admit, she's done an amazing and seamless job. Everyone who was invited has shown up and we've been handing out donuts—like Maisey's Maple and Bacon, the OTT (a strawberry jam-filled donut, stuffed with cream cheese and topped with lavender sprinkles), and my favorite, the Big Bad Boss Hog. This one is insane: filled with chocolate and marshmallows, with a graham cracker dusting, rolled in cinnamon and sugar, then deep fried.

No wonder the local fire department had shown up and brought their ambulance crew with them. There could be heart attacks today.

Grabbing the phone Ari's presenting to me, I snap the pic, then go back to my current role in the kitchen. We'd arrived a little before seven this morning to set up in the park, with Ari barking orders so we could get the photos needed on the shot list done before we got busy. It was a breeze to do because of how organized it was. We'd gotten the whole list ticked off in less than fifteen minutes, high-fived, and then had enough time to throw back coffee before everyone started showing up.

This is clearly Ari's thing. I'm watching her talk to people, milling around the various cliques, hopping in like she belongs. She's the perfect Southern hostess—you'd think she'd invited everyone over to her place for morning tea the way she handles herself. You would never guess this was the girl who was in the parking lot with her skirt over her head last night. No, she looks like she went to Miss Patricia Altshul's School for the Southern Belle.

The door to the truck flies open. "This is going so well, and everyone's having a blast." Ari's face is bright, her smile wide. She climbs the steps to join me inside, closing the door behind her.

I'm busy organizing our last round of donut samples and preparing the plate for the live cross that's yet to be done with the local news station. There's still more photos to be taken as well, which I'll get around to momentarily. After my distraction leaves, that is.

Ari leans against the counter beside me, scrolling through her phone and tapping away.

"Don't forget Freya gave us that list so you can make sure everyone's tagged."

She stops what she's doing, her finger hovering mid-tap

56

over the keyboard. "You're afraid this is going to be like Reid's sixteenth birthday?" she challenges me.

A smile plays on my lips. I remember alright, and yes, maybe a little afraid. It was a big deal for Reid to have a sixteenth birthday, mostly because he's Reid and liked celebrating himself back then. And like I said, the Shannons know how to do a birthday.

This particular year, he'd managed to make his little sister angry right at the same time her mom asked her to be the one to invite all of his friends over for his party. Reid had been excited about it for weeks, and his parents had made plans to order pizzas and let Reid have a night where everyone could sleep over if they wanted and stay up as late as they dared.

When I arrived, it was five in the evening, but the party was starting at six. At six thirty, no one else had come, so we figured they were running late. By seven thirty, Reid was getting antsy. It was around eight thirty that Ari let it drop she'd never invited anyone.

I've blocked most of the rest of the night from memory. There was yelling, screaming, tears...and I think Ari was grounded. But I do remember having two pizzas all to myself.

"Yes, I am," I shoot back, winking. "Just kidding. You're doing great. Maisey's texted me already to say she's watching her social media go off and she loves it."

Ari beams. "That's so good to hear. Freya sent me a few notes as well. She's really happy." Ari tilts her chin in the direction of the camera crew. "Now we just have to get the interview out of the way and we're good as gold."

She turns her focus back on her phone, tap, tap, tapping away. I watch her fingers fly across the keyboard and listen in as she talks to herself while answering comments. I don't even realize how long I've been staring at her until she freezes and turns to me.

"What?" Deep, brown eyes hold me hostage. A hand flies

to the corner of her mouth. "Oh no. I've got bacon on my lips, don't I?"

"I thought you did, but turns out it's the way the light was hitting your face." Busted, I turn away and play it off. I grab the plate of donuts for the TV crew and slide it toward her. "Here, all ready for ya."

She grins that beautiful magnetic smile of hers as she pushes her hair back from her face. "Thanks. I'm going to do another round before the influencers leave, make sure they have all the info they need, then I'll get the crew over." She opens the door, turning back to me before she steps out. "We still work really well together, Carter. I'm having fun."

With that, she gives me one last smile as she hops out of the truck and goes back to work.

I gotta admit. I'm having a blast. Her presence gives me comfort like a snug blanket with our past the thread holding it together. For the first time in years, I'm feeling grounded and connected. I can't help but think it's because of Ari.

But then again, I'm just a dude making some donuts. A dude making donuts who feels guilty because of a rogue moment in a darkroom years ago.

I know, it's confusing, isn't it? Do I have feelings for her, do I not...trust me. It's confusing for me, too. And I've been dealing with this for years. But how am I supposed to act when her brother would break me in half if I broke her heart?

Playing barista, I take orders at the window, then make a few more lattes and flat whites, handing them out in takeaway cups to our morning partygoers. While the small but mighty crowd is dispersing, I notice a little boy hanging out on the outskirts of our cluster. He's watching everyone with keen interest, so he's probably with one of the influencers, right? I wave him over, pointing to the leftover donuts on the tray in front of me.

As he walks over, I notice Ari's been corralled by the local fire department and is chatting with a few of the firefighters. They probably know her through Reid; he knows everyone around here. I know I shouldn't feel like this, but dang gone if I don't want to be over there with her. As the thought washes through me, I chastise myself, feeling like a cat who needs to pee on his territory—only she's not my territory. I saw to that a long time ago, and something in her voice last night told me she still feels the sting of it, too.

Did I tell her we weren't going to kiss again after the moment alone at school? Yeah, I did. But I didn't want to tell her that—I had to. Part of it was that in no way was I going to cross the line Reid had drawn for us. But there's another part, too.

The little boy's made his way to me, and stands outside the truck expectantly. I nod my head in the direction of the plate.

"Help yourself."

His eyes widen. "Really?"

I nod and go to hand him a few napkins, but I accidentally knock over two of the coffees I'd made. I jump back to escape the hot liquid, then turn my attention back to my new little friend. Still clutching the napkins in my hand, I hold them out thinking he'll take one. Maybe two.

No, he's got other plans.

Grabbing his backpack, he swings it in front of him, unzipping it and shoving all the napkins inside. Small hands come up to the counter as he grabs the plate and proceeds to empty all of its contents inside his backpack.

"Oh, wait." Maybe he didn't understand. My boy has just swiped twelve donuts. "Did you want them all?"

Big blue eyes, like bright sparkling sapphires, blink in my direction. "It's for my mommy and my little sister. They're hungry and I said I'd try to find us something to eat."

I look around but don't see anyone mom-like standing nearby with a small child, like a little sister. "Are they close?"

59

He nods, pointing across the park. "That way."

I follow where he indicates. There's a playground full of people, a ball field with a game about to start, and what looks like an old bridge just beyond that must lead to another part of the park. They're probably over at the ball game, and he's trying to be the "big man" in charge of his family. It's a good effort. I like this kid.

We were going to have to get rid of the food anyway, so I let it go. If he wants all the donuts, he can have them. "Enjoy it, bud. I hope your mom and sister like them, too."

"Thanks." He turns on his heel and jogs off, right as Ari comes skipping over to the truck.

"Who was that?" she asks, watching the boy as he races across the park.

"A masked donut thief." Chuckling, I shrug and turn my attention to the plate I'd been saving for the live cross. "I guess it's time?"

Ari's eyes dance with excitement. "My palms are sweaty."

"Don't shake hands, then."

She pulls a face while play-swiping at my arm. "Shut up. I'm nervous, that's all."

I grab her arms, holding her elbows. "You are going to kill it. Like the time in eighth grade when you had to give an oral report to all of the science classes. You were mesmerizing. I never knew the Big Bang Theory could be so interesting."

Looking over her shoulder, I can see the crew making their way over to the truck. The reporter gives us a hand signal telling us they're about to start filming. The cameraman waves a hand in the air, signaling Ari as well.

"There's my cue. I'm to be at the window serving them donuts when they walk up." She smiles, steeling herself for what's about to come next. "You're right. I got this. What could go wrong? It's only donuts."

I hate when someone says what could go wrong because something always does.

As the light comes on for the TV crew and the live cross begins, Ari turns on her heel and takes a step over to the counter. Her job is simple: she holds out the plate to them, and they take the donuts and eat them.

So simple, right? But those coffees I knocked over? I haven't had a chance to clean them up yet.

Ari takes two steps and then she's down. It's a slow motion tumble with her hand clawing the air wanting to grab anything that could save her as she slips onto the floor. Like last night's fall, her feet go in the air again, but her destructive right hand flies out, almost as if it's detached. It takes out the other two coffees on the counter, and I watch in horror as that stinking bracelet on her wrist clanks against the steel of the counter when her hand connects with the plate of donuts.

The last of the donuts we have with us for the crew to sample.

The plate slides with her, but somehow I'm able to thrust myself on top of her, grabbing the plate and stopping it from going off the edge. I push myself with such force that I end up dropping right on top of Ari. Let me tell you, she's not the softest pillow to land on, but she's the best.

I'm also aware there's still a live cross happening and they can't stop it. Underneath me, Ari groans, rolling over. We're nose to nose, and her face is white as she pushes me off. In less than two seconds flat, she manages to pull herself up—her white shirt and khaki pants now covered in coffee, chocolate, and mud—lean on the counter, flash a smile as wide as the Blue Ridge Mountains for the cameras, and get back into her role.

"Ta da! When you get your morning fix from The Sweet Spot, we'll also make sure to give you a show."

The gathered crowd erupts into loud cheers with Ari

bowing and waving a hand in the air. "Thank you. We'll be leaving soon, so if you want another slip and fall with your coffee break, I'm your gal!"

Turning away from the camera for a moment, she lets out a huge breath of relief, looking down at where I'm still lying at her feet. "I guess you had a spill?" she asks.

I'm impressed. She manages her words through gritted teeth, but somehow manages a smile for the cameras. Skills.

The reporter motions for Ari to come outside. Nodding, she steps over me, opening the door to go, but throws me one last look before she does. I know that look. She's fighting to keep from laughing while I'm wishing I could pull her back into my arms again.

Right then I understand the reason why I was drawn back to Lake Lorelei, to coming home. Watching her oh-so-effort-lessly skip out of the truck and fall into an interview, I'm impressed—but I've always known she has it in her. She's the one person who my thoughts always come back to, no matter where I'm living or who I'm dating.

It's always been her. Ari Shannon is home.

Now I need to get her to see it, too.

CHAPTER 7

Ari

"I've decided that bracelet on your arm? It's got to go."

Carter's words cut through me like a hot knife slicing through butter. I'm stowing the last of our utensils away and locking the cabinets in the truck so we can get outta dodge, and can feel his eyes burning a hole through me. Glancing down at my favorite accessory, I shake my head.

"No can do." I take the bracelet off, make my way to the front seat of the truck, and hide it in a side pocket of my purse. Is it crazy I don't want him to see that I still have that charm in my possession? I think it's sweet and nostalgic, but I also don't want to answer any questions right now as to why I have it still. "We're not throwing it into the lake, Carter."

Stretching my arms over my head, I close my eyes tightly and let out a giant sigh-scream, one that's not for the faint of heart. When I open my eyes, Carter is staring at me, his jaw slack and his eyes as wide as a dinner plate. Or the donut on the top of the truck. Could be either.

"What was that?"

"Stress release." I laugh as I finish securing cabinets for our ride back. "The last twenty-four hours have been intense. You can't tell me otherwise."

Carter's emerald eyes sparkle in the light. "I have no desire to go up against you on that one. But hey, we managed to navigate through all of it, didn't we?"

"We did. I have to admit, there were times I was reminded of how well we worked together when we did the school paper."

"Right?" Carter hops out of the truck momentarily to put our bags away for the ride, but is back inside in a flash and closing the space between us. "We work really well together, I'd say."

"We do." I grin and my stomach rumbles like an eighteen wheeler on the turnpike. "Wow. I'm starving."

"I can make us something to eat?" Carter waves his hand around the kitchen. "We're in a food truck. I made sure to pack some extra food in case we wanted something more than donuts and coffee."

Of course he did. I bet he's also got a first aid kit and fire extinguisher in his backpack, too.

"If you don't mind whipping something up, I won't say no."

I hadn't noticed how close together our bodies had become. Watching him, I'm mesmerized. I *had* noticed Carter not-so-subtly checking me out today—especially when I was talking to Reid's friend who's on the local fire truck. His eyes are swallowing me whole at this very moment, and I don't want it to stop. He reaches out, tucking a stray piece of my hair behind my ear—a move he's used before. The warmth of his fingers as they slide across my face sends a tingle down into my fingertips. There's an emotional charge firing off between us—but the moment's cut short when someone knocks on the door to the truck.

"Excuse me." The door opens and a young woman sticks

her head inside. "I'm sorry to bother you. I'm looking for the person who gave my son all of the donuts?"

Turning to Carter, my head tilts. "Do you know anything about this?"

His cheeks flush red, which surprises me. Carter Snowden embarrassed? Stepping forward, he shoves his hands in his pockets like a little boy about to be scolded and looks down at his feet.

"Yes, ma'am. That was me."

Her eyes rock back and forth between us. My stomach clenches with fear. Please for the love of everything don't let that child have food poisoning.

Yes, sometimes I'm a bit dramatic.

I needn't have worried. Her features erupt in a smile. "Thank you on behalf of me, Henry, and Ella for the donuts. It's not been an easy time for us lately; we're in the middle of a life upheaval." Tired, dull hazel eyes are crinkled in the corners, worry etched across her face. Beside her, a boy's hand is tucked in her own and another small figure is busy wrapping herself around her mother's leg.

"It was my pleasure," Carter murmurs, leaning out the door holding his hand up to Henry for a high five. "Good to see you again, bud. Are you back for a tour?"

The two clap their hands together, and Henry looks at his mom for approval. She nods as he leaps up the step and into the truck to join Carter.

Emerging from the truck, I join Henry's mom outside. Behind me Carter and his little buddy start banging around in the kitchen.

"I'm glad you caught us, we're about to leave." I look down at the cherub wrapped around her leg. "So you're Ella?"

Blonde curls bob up and down, her face pressed away from me. Making eye contact with her mom, she smiles. It's bright and wide, a stark contrast to what her eyes tell me.

"She's shy, but thankful as well." Looking down at her feet, the mom shuffles in place. "My name's Laura."

"Ari." I point a thumb at the truck behind me. "We're in for the day from Lake Lorelei, promoting this truck for a friend."

"Lake Lorelei." Her expression flashes recognition. "You know, I have an aunt who lives near there. I've not spoken to my own family in a very long time." She shrugs, dragging her eyes away from mine. "Family can be tricky. Especially when you fall on hard times."

My senses are tingling, making me suspect that there is so much more to this woman and her story. I've always had the ability to read through people, you know? Like an empath, I swear I can feel people's energy. Hers is loving and sweet, but dripping with disappointment.

"Lake Lorelei is a great place to be. One of the best things about it is the way our community comes together to help each other out when we need it. I feel like bigger cities can't give you the warmth a small town can."

Laura nods as Henry bounces back outside with Carter hot on his heels.

"Look, Mom!" Henry excitedly holds up a few of our take-away bags. "Carter found some food that would go to waste, so he made us a whole bunch of sandwiches!"

From the sound of his voice, you'd have thought they'd won the lottery. My fragile heart is breaking into a million tiny shattered pieces.

"You didn't have to do that." Laura's voice is stern, but laced with gratitude.

"We had the food for the event." Carter holds out a fist to Henry. "So your boy has made excellent use of our leftovers."

Watching the two fist bump, I sneak a look at Laura and see her eyes welling with tears. She shakes her head and laughs, throwing a last smile our way.

"Thank you." Her eyes dart between us. "I mean it from the bottom of my heart."

Waving, they say goodbye—Ella even managing a quick wave as they start across the park with Henry still clutching the bag tightly in his hands.

* * *

"Cheeseburger with fries, please. Cooked medium. Side of mayo." I hand the waitress my menu and hold out an expectant hand to Carter. "Your turn."

"I'll have what my date is having." He wiggles his eyebrows, making me laugh. Of course Carter would give away our food to someone who needs it. I'm fine with it, but we were both still starving so we stopped for a quick bite before getting on the road.

And don't think it slips past me he said I was his date.

Sitting in a booth at the window, we both stare outside. My thoughts keep going back to Henry's family. Sitting back in the booth, I put my hands on the table and tap it a few times.

Carter turns in his seat. "Four taps?"

"Yes. Why?"

Did Carter's cheeks just go bright red? "Four taps means you're stumped."

I narrow my eyes. "You remember?

He tosses his head back and laughs. "Of course I do! Like I know two taps means 'come on, let's go.' Two taps was always a code Reid and I used."

He's got to be joking. He knows my taps?

"I had no clue. How did you guys use it?"

"Reid uses it when he wants to get out of a situation. We've done it since he caught on to you doing it." He snickers. "Two taps means we are outta here, as he says."

"So." Inquiring green eyes stare back at me. "Four taps?"

I shrug it off. "Meeting Henry and his mom has got me thinking."

"About?"

"Next steps. Going back to Lake Lorelei and dealing with my job."

Carter grunts, causing me to cross my arms across my chest.

"And what does that mean?"

"I'm surprised." His cell phone pings, signaling a text coming through. He glances at the screen before rolling his eyes and putting it down again. It's probably his real date from a few nights ago. Whatever.

"Why surprised?" Glutton for punishment, party of one, please.

"The Ari I know would be fighting a little harder. I don't know, thinking outside the box. You're a very clever woman, Ari. Always have been. When the school board wanted to stop the music program at school due to lack of funding, you were the one who got a group together to raise money to keep the band going."

I smile at the memory. "'Twas one of my finest hours."

"Pat yourself on the back, you still deserve it." He flashes his charismatic grin my way. Pulling me in like a fish on a hook. "Maybe you can step up here and do something about it."

Sighing, I lean my arms on the table. "Unless I can find an investor for the paper, one who comes with experience as an editor and wants to be in charge of a motley crew of reporters in Lake Lorelei, we're dead in the water. Actually, I take it back. We're dead in print, but alive digitally."

"We both know Liz Donnelly won't be reading the paper on her iPad anytime soon," he jokes as the waitress slides our food in front of us. Taking a bite of his burger, his phone

68

pings again. Without looking this time, he turns it off and shoves it on the seat beside him.

"Are you avoiding someone?"

"Well, yes and no." He chews thoughtfully for a few moments. "When I was in Paris for school, I met someone who is opening a restaurant in New York City. At the time, I was drawn to all the shiny things. I wanted to be in Italy, New York, Paris, LA...all of it and everywhere. Lance is friends with one of my teachers. He puts money into restaurants, helping them grow and become the best they can be. When we met, we got along instantly. He told me he'd be in touch when he found something I may want to consider."

"I take it he's found something?"

Carter nods, and my stomach lurches. "It's in New York. City."

"Wow, Carter." My burger suddenly doesn't taste very good at all. "That's a once in a lifetime opportunity. What are you going to do?

"I don't know." Carter turns his head, facing the window again. "I just got back home and have my own dreams, but an offer like this doesn't come along every day."

Pushing my fries around on my plate, something inside me spirals. It's singing "told you so" as if I'd let down my guard a teensy bit and was now being reprimanded.

Of course he'll go to New York. He just told me how much he wants to.

"Sounds like the world's your oyster." My turn to wiggle my eyebrows and try to lighten the moment.

"I don't know what to do. I've made a commitment to Maisey for The Sweet Spot, so I have at least a year to see out. It sounds like by the time I'm done with the contract for the food truck, the restaurant in NYC would be fitted out and ready for me then, anyway." He snorts. "The world may be my oyster, but I'm ready to clam up."

Carter shoves a fistful of fries in his mouth, chewing them aggressively.

"You need to calm down; you'll give yourself lockjaw."

"It's a great opportunity, don't get me wrong, I'm just not sure I want that dream anymore. It's like it doesn't fit any longer with who I want to be."

Now *that* I understand. "You also want to make your own mark on the world."

"Like you, I love working with food, and I really like being a fireman, too." He lifts his eyes to meet mine. "And yes, I do want to make my mark on the world. I don't know how I'll do it, I don't know where I'll do it. But I do know my dad would have wanted this for me."

"He'd be so proud of you, Carter."

Carter opens his mouth to say something right when something across the street catches my eye.

"Isn't that Henry and his family?" I nod my head toward the window.

Carter follows my gaze. Standing in line across the street we see Henry, Ella, and Laura. Above them, a sign hangs: Community Food Bank.

We're silent for the next ten minutes as we finish our meals. To be honest, I barely finish mine. Between Carter's reveal and seeing how hard it is for Henry and his family, my psyche is in pain.

As we're waiting at the cashier's stand to pay our check, I wander over to the newspaper racks. Touching the paper I relish the moment. I'm also the girl who loves to read paperback books, but I have to admit that my e-reader is always close to my side, too. Maybe going digital won't be as bad as I'm thinking, but I digress.

As Carter joins me, I point to the headline. It touts a new influx of cash for the local speedway and reveals a scandal centered around a local politician. "Why can't the headlines show that?" I tilt my chin in the direction of the food bank across the street. I can't see Henry any longer, but the line still snakes down the block.

"Why isn't this in the local news? The community needs to know they have to step up to help their own."

Carter's arm snakes around my shoulders, pulling me close. Not a move that is foreign to me—he used to do this same move to both Reid and I when we would hang out together. Only this time when he does, it has a different meaning. I like having his weight against me like this as we walk together. I can smell the fresh scent of the soap he uses when I rest my head on his shoulder. My stomach shudders as if thousands of butterflies have decided to take flight at once.

Carter Snowden is getting under my skin—and in the most wonderful way possible.

We walk down the street, Carter's arm still draped around my shoulders. I'm not pushing him off. I don't want to. The world's been moving at an epic rate around me lately, change coming and going at lightning fast speed. It's nice to be with someone who knows me as well as he does.

"Ari! Carter! Wait up."

Turning, we see Henry crossing the street, with his family keeping pace behind him. Laura's head hangs low.

"Henry, what are the chances we keep seeing you?" Carter laughs, kneeling down to talk to the boy. "What are you doing?"

"We got our free food and now we're going to find a place to sleep," he says with childlike honesty.

Laura pulls her eyes to mine. "It's not like he makes it sound," she stammers. "I mean, yes, it has been tough. But we're not going to be as rough tonight as we have been, are we, kids?"

Two small blond heads nod in agreement.

"We're staying in a motel tonight." Henry's eyes are wide

71

and excited. "Mommy called auntie Rae and she's coming to get us tomorrow."

I look at Laura. "You called her?"

"I sure did, right after I met you." She grins, light starting to creep back into her eyes. "I've been very obstinate about our situation, thinking I'd be able to pull us out of it on my own, but I realized today I need help. Aunt Rae is coming to get us in the morning."

"So you'll be in Lake Lorelei?" If I sound hopeful it's because I am. There's something about Laura I really like, and these two kids are adorable. The lake is a place where the eclectic are known to gather, folks who are looking to start over or get a second chance...why not for them, too?

"We will be. I hope we can see each other there? Maybe after I get a job," she says with half a laugh.

"You and me both, Laura." I reach in my bag and grab a piece of paper and a pen, scribbling my phone number for her. I start to hand it to her but take it back and add another number as well. "The first one is my cell. Let me know once you're settled and I'll come by. Show you guys around. The second number is for my friend Maisey. She owns a cafe in town and I know she's often hiring servers; they seem to come and go seasonally. She may have a spot for you, so give her a shout."

Behind us, Carter's entertaining Henry and Ella, pulling faces and talking in fake accents. Their laughter falls around us like warm sunshine.

"They're happy because I'm happy. The last few weeks have been very humbling to say the least." She lowers her voice, stepping close, and whispers, "Their father passed away suddenly, leaving us in major debt. He had re-mortgaged our home and never told me, and there were bad business deals. We lost everything, including the house. I was too proud to ask for help; instead we've couch-surfed with friends for a few weeks. I wanted to fix it for us. I didn't want to admit I can't do it alone."

I put my hand on her arm. "May I ask what made you change your mind?"

"Him." She nods toward Henry. "When he went out on his own today to find food for us, it broke me. He wants to be the man of the family now. I got scared I would be robbing him of his childhood. Then I met you, and when you said you were from the lake I took it as a sign."

"When the signs flash that bright, you have to be open to them, don't you?" I grin, looking at my watch. "We should hit the road so we don't get caught in rush hour around Asheville."

Carter and I say our goodbyes, with one last promise to talk in a few weeks' time once Laura is settled, Carter even promising tours of the fire station for everyone.

We're both silent as we leave Charlotte in the rearview mirror, but it's not long before Carter finds his voice again.

"You have the power in you to bring stories like theirs to the light, you know."

I turn in my seat as much as my seat belt will allow me to face him. "What do you mean?"

"The newspaper, silly. You can use it to tell stories like theirs."

"I only do food. I'm not sure I could write something that packs that much punch."

"You never give yourself enough credit. I know you can do it. If you won't believe in yourself right now, allow me to step in and do it for ya." Leaning forward, he taps the dashboard three times, winking. "Ah-ha moment, anyone?"

"Ha ha moment, more like it." I look out the window, watching the scenery flow past like a moving picture box. "I don't know, Carter. I wouldn't want to get it wrong, you know?"

He snickers behind the wheel. "You always have to get it right, don't you? Maybe this once you should let caution be thrown to the wind and think about what I'm saying. You're not only a food writer, you're a journalist. You know how to write the hard hitting stories, and I know for a fact that you're a wicked editor in chief."

"Flatterer." I bat my lashes.

"Seriously. And I'll help. I can take pictures to go with the story, if you want. We make a good team, me and you."

He's right, but if he's in New York, then the team is split. "You talk a big game for someone who has an offer in his texts right now to open his own restaurant in NYC next year. What do I do then? Hire a new photographer?"

Carter goes quiet. It's the kind of silence that screams. This whole New York thing is hitting a nerve for him, I can tell.

We cover the last part of the drive in an hour. Carter has the dubious honor of dropping me off at my place so he can take The Sweet Spot back to Maisey's. Not only does he pull right up the driveway for me, instead of dumping on the street like Reid would, Carter also leaps out of the truck and grabs my suitcase for me, walking up to the porch.

"Thanks. And thank you for the last two days." I smile as I reach in my pocket for my house keys. "It's been fun and enlightening."

The corner of his mouth twitches; I know he's holding back a grin. "Enlightening?"

He steps closer to me and points to my cheek. "Ari, what is that?"

My hand flies up in a flash. "Could be so many things. Do I have a piece of gummy bear stuck on my face?"

Gentle hands with soft calluses reach up and push away whatever it is, his fingers faltering at my jawline. Carter pinches my chin between his thumb and forefinger, softly stroking my skin.

In any normal circumstance, I would not want to do this on my front porch. Small town, remember? Anyone could go by and see us, and if it's Connie, we're in trouble. Everyone will know that Reid's best friend was on his little sister's porch, with them standing a little closer than they needed to be.

Only I don't want him to stop. I want his fingers to caress my skin and twine through my hair. I want to stand on my tiptoes and cover his mouth with mine, and let him know I'm feeling more than I should be. A lot more.

His gaze is on my mouth, his jaw hardening when I bite my lower lip. I see what I'm doing to him, and it's coming back and slamming into my body tenfold.

Tilting his head, he leans in closer, his breath on my cheek as something somewhere nearby pings loudly. Carter stops, the moment on pause, before he slowly begins to lean even closer. My body sparks with full electric anticipation.

The ping sounds off again; this time Carter clenches his eyes closed and mutters a few expletives (not fit for sharing) under his breath. The pinging won't stop because his phone is ringing in his pocket. Woeful eyes meet mine. Carter grabs the phone, and with a look of resignation, presses a button.

"Hey, Reid." He's quiet as he listens to Reid talking. I'm only getting Carter's side of things, but I know how they're going to go. "Yep. Yep. You got it. Dropping her off now, she's right here... Okay, I'll tell her. See you in a few."

I had taken the opportunity while he was on the phone to unlock my door and step inside. Shivers may be coursing all through me, but I have enough wits about me to pull back. That, and Reid calling, of course.

"Thanks again for dropping me off." I wave a hand toward

the truck. "Go and be free. You've earned your keep for the day."

"You sure?" Carter's look of confusion doesn't escape me. "I told Reid we might hang out when I got back, but seeing as we live together right now, I never expected him to take me up on it."

"He can be pushy when he wants to be. I have laundry to do anyway and jobs to look for."

Carter backs down the steps, then starts toward the truck, stopping once more to turn back. "Thanks for listening. And thanks for talking to me. There's a lot happening right now and it's nice to have someone I can talk to who I feel so secure with."

"Like a blanket," I joke.

His eyes darken. "Not really."

We both stand in our places watching the other with interest—me at the door and him with one foot in the truck. He taps the top of the truck twice, grinning as he does so, before hopping in and backing out of the driveway.

Catching a glimpse of the donuts on top of the truck as he makes his way down the street, one thing has become abundantly clear.

I don't want Carter disappearing out of my life ever again.

CHAPTER 8

Carter

"This one is the best one. No wait. This one is."

Maisey sits between me and Reid at the counter of the Red Bird flicking through images on my camera. Reid was insistent he see me as soon as possible, so I encouraged him to join me when I dropped off the truck to Maisey. In the back of my mind I was hoping I might be brave enough to ask him about Ari, but we'll see.

"These are great, Carter." Maisey clicks through more images I snapped during our set up. The early morning sunlight in Charlotte was excellent for our photo session, the natural light adding oomph to the photos. We took plenty of pictures of donuts, perfect for Maisey and Freya to use for their marketing efforts. Judging by the smile playing on her lips, I think Maisey's happy with the results.

"How can you guys take all of those photos and not get hungry?" Reid shakes his head, talking between bites of his BLT.

"You're breathing heavily in my ear, Reid." Maisey laughs, nudging him with her shoulder.

"It's a good BLT." Shrugging, he indicates to the camera with his sandwich-holding hand. "That's, like, the umpteenth picture with Ari, dude. Was it necessary to get her in so many photos?"

I feel the heat rise to my cheeks, threatening to give away my emotions. "She's the influencer for The Sweet Spot—right Maisey?"

Bright green eyes flash my way before turning back to the camera in her hand. "She is. Besides the live cross incident..."

"So good," Reid chortles. "But she recovered well." He leans around Maisey and points to me. "It's a Shannon trait, you know. We bounce back."

"Whatever." The guy has always made me laugh. We've been best friends for so long—probably why my palms sweat buckets when I think of telling him I'd like to be more than friends with his sister.

Glancing back to the camera, I watch as Maisey clicks through a slew of snaps rapidly, cutting her eyes in my direction. All Ari. Ari holding donuts, Ari with the coffee. Ari laughing as she tells me to stop taking pictures.

Clicking the camera's off button, Maisey hands it back to me, narrowing her eyes and giving me a knowing look.

"They're awesome photos and so telling." She leans back in her seat, crossing her arms. "You're a triple treat, Carter. A photographer, a chef, and a fireman. A modern day renaissance man."

"When Mom took off, and before Dad fell down the bottle, he showed me what to do. My dad was a staff photographer for a newspaper in Washington D.C. years ago."

"Huh. I never knew." Maisey nudges me with her elbow. "You've got that talent, honestly. Some of those photos are more raw than commercial."

Again, green eyes pull me in, staring me down and reading my thoughts.

"I like to go with the moment, and considering we had only twenty minutes to get those shots in before the event started, I think we delivered." Tossing an arm around Maisey, I pull her close. "If we need to take more, let me know. I'm happy to take extra shots for you."

"I bet you are," she mutters under her breath. Down the counter a few tables are waiting at the register to pay, so she hops up and jogs over leaving me alone with Reid.

"It's cool you and your dad got to fix things before he passed away." Reid slides my way, taking over Maisey's stool. "There was a time when I never would have expected to hear you talking about him with fondness."

"You bore witness to all of it. The drinking, me being a parent for my parent, his acerbic tongue." I shudder at the memory but recover quickly. "It took a lot, but we got there in the end. The best gift ever was when he chose to get sober after I graduated."

"What made him finally do it?"

"Seeing me standing with you and your family. He never felt good enough, especially after Mom left us high and dry. But he told me when he saw your family surrounding you—us—on graduation day, and saw the camaraderie and love there, he realized he'd missed that time with me. A few days later he went into rehab." A warmth spreads through my chest at the memory. "I got to know my dad again and spent a few years being friends with him before he died. That's the best thing ever."

Even though he's focused on his sandwich, Reid's listening. In rare moments, the guy can be thoughtful, and this is one of those times. Like I said, he was front row for a lot of the drama in my house when I was growing up.

"I'm glad he did, too." He picks up his cup and clinks mine. "To our history. I'll always have your back."

If there was ever an opportunity, now's the time. My

stomach dips in anticipation. Opening my mouth, I'm deter-mined to bring up Ari—but Reid keeps going.

"Hope you don't mind, but Dylan and her cousin are coming over for dinner this week. Thought there was a connection for you and Louise?"

"Is it for me or is this for you?" There's nothing inside me wanting another double date with Reid, Dylan, and her cousin. If we swapped the cousin for Ari, we'd be talking. I'm serious when I ask him who the date's for, though. I have my suspicions.

"Of course this date is for you," he says as he chokes on his sandwich. "Dylan said her cousin is really into you. You had fun the other night, right?"

"Well, I enjoyed watching you and Dylan spar all night, if that's what you mean."

Dylan's wit is rapid-fire, and honest to goodness, Reid is no match for it. The tension is thick between these two. You can cut it with a knife.

"Pffft." Reid finishes the last bite and shoves the empty plate across the counter. "Dylan's a pain in my you-know-what, but I owe her one."

Pulling his wallet out of his back pocket, Reid grabs a twenty-dollar bill, placing it on the counter. "Gotta run. I'm going to let Dylan know it's a yes. Cool?"

Without waiting for an answer, he's gone. Why? Because he knows I have his back, so of course I'll be his wingman for his double date.

"Did I hear you two organizing another night out?"

Maisey's back, sliding onto the stool next to me, reaching for my camera.

"Whether I want to or not." I swivel in my seat to face her. I feel like I should let her in on the secret. "He thinks he's setting me up, but in reality I'm his wingman."

"Oh? Do tell."

"I've been watching him with Dylan since I've been back. He's got it bad for her, but he doesn't want to admit it." Smug, I grab my coffee cup and hold it in the air. "Tell me I'm wrong."

My needs are satiated when Maisey shakes her head no. "Can't say you're wrong about that. Reid has a huge crush and it's funny as all get out to witness. You know, one thing I've learned over the years is how to read people. Especially from working here with my mom. Restaurants are great for understanding human behavior."

"A case of if these walls could talk?"

"Oh yeah," she says with a chuckle, before turning in her seat to face me. She's turned the camera back on and is flipping through the photos, landing on a string that are all taken of one subject. "And if this camera could talk, what would it say, Carter?"

Inquiring eyes want to know. I'm on the hot seat. "It would say, 'Carter you are the man.'"

"Mmhmmm. Anything else?"

"Nope." Uh-uh. Not going here.

"Carter."

I stare at her, she stares at me. It's a standoff at the counter of the Red Bird. She's patient, though. It's like she's trained for this. She stares at her fingernails then sits back to look at me again. I hold my gaze; I don't want to buckle.

But I do. I pinch my eyes closed. "What?"

"I know." She leans close to me, whispering. The sounds of clinking glasses and rattles of the busy cafe seem miles away. "I watched the two of you exchange hearts a long time ago, Carter."

"I have no clue what you're talking about."

"It's not a coincidence your motel room was canceled."

My jaw smacks the counter. "You did that?"

"I sure did." Maisey sits back in her chair and twiddles her fingers together with glee. "I saw the fireworks between the two of you when you were younger. One thing my mother taught me was when you see there's a chance you can bring good into your immediate world, you do it. In this case, I bore witness to it, so I decided to meddle."

"Maisey, you butted in. On. Purpose."

"You bet I did." She hops up, making her way to the other side of the counter. "More coffee?"

I watch her refill my cup as I let her confession sink in. I want to be mad, but I can't be. This woman has done something that took some guts. "I guess we're lucky that she didn't leave me in the truck to fry in the heat, then, aren't we?"

"I'd never let it get that far." She chuckles as she goes down the counter, refilling the empty cups of other customers nearby. "I think you need to go get her, stop screwing around. You want her to be the one that got away?"

Pinching my lips together, I look down at my hands, gripping my coffee mug. I have no comeback. I drag my eyes from the cup to meet Maisey's.

"Oh." Her eyes grow wide. "You already think that, don't you?"

What I can't say to Maisey is, of course I do. How can someone like me, who comes from such a broken home, be a match for someone like Ari? Growing up I saw the utopia that was her life compared to the train wreck that was mine.

"Maisey, I can't go there. I have so many reasons."

Her eyebrows hitch. "Like Reid?"

"That's one."

She rolls her eyes. "Please. You two are adults now. I think a childhood promise can be renegotiated."

"I'm not good enough for her in that way, Maisey." The words hurt to say out loud, but it feels good to get it off my chest. "Trust me, I've tried to be. You compliment me for being talented, and what's my response? That I challenged myself because I wanted to be better for her."

"Then what's the problem?"

"Why do you think I was always at the Shannon's house? Part of the reason was to get away from my own insanity. Reid helped me hide my dad's illness."

"You took on a lot at a young age. It doesn't mean you're not good enough." She shakes her head. "No. It means you've got scars, but scars heal. You know, I see things." She tilts her head, squinting her eyes as if lost in thought. "I see what others don't see. I see when Ari looks at you, she does it with pure joy and love in her eyes. And guess what? It's reflected right back in yours. You two have such a deep connection. It's been years since you've seen each other and you both fell back into step immediately. Doesn't happen that way for everyone, my friend. Don't let her slip past you."

While she has a point, there's so much Maisey doesn't know. Like the fact I've been the one over the years on the receiving end of the calls from Reid. When he'd fill me in on the latest in his life, but also being a good big brother, he'd keep me up-to-date on Ari, too. I heard about her heartbreaks over the years and all the things Reid wanted to do to the guys who hurt her.

Of course, there's also that pang deep in my gut knowing I'm one of the guys who caused her heartache so many years ago.

"I can see by the storm cloud crossing your face you're doing some thinking." Maisey props herself against the counter, wiping down salt shakers. "Look, if you don't think it's something worth pursuing, then fine. I'm sorry I meddled and tried to force you two together. I think it was kismet, to be honest, but if it's not your thing, that's cool."

A bell sounds in the kitchen, signaling Maisey. "My final

thought for you—make sure you look closely at that bracelet on her wrist the next time she's wearing it."

She disappears, like an insane but well-meaning fairy godmother leaving me with a lot to think about.

CHAPTER 9

Ari

Have I been avoiding Carter for the last few days since we got back? You bet. It's not that I don't want to see him, it's that...I don't want to see him. When he's around, my mind melts and my body follows suit. The overwhelm I'm feeling has taken over my every thought.

It's like my suppressed crush from my teenage years has leapt out of the lake like the Loch Ness Monster. Every day since the moment on the porch I've daydreamed about my lips on Carter's. My lips on his neck, his lips on mine. I want to pull his body close and feel his heartbeat while I run my fingers through his hair...

"Ari? Do you want me to still get photos of Laura, Henry, and Ella together or just Laura now?"

"Yes, please. Thanks, Carter."

I can't lie. When Laura called me and told me she was in town, I decided to go for it like Carter and I'd talked about on the drive home. I called Morris, after I had delivered my write-up on The Sweet Spot, and asked if I could have a front page article for the last edition. I was shocked he said yes, but he liked the pitch.

Now I just needed to make sure I had a good photographer on board, cause Morris had already let the one he had on staff go. Who do you think was the first person that came to mind?

Seeing how at ease the small family is with Carter, I know I made the right choice. Even if being near him means my hormones are firing off on all cylinders, I'm willing to do it to get the story out. Our community needs to be aware of the situation a lot of our lower-income neighbors are in—and I'm grateful Laura agreed.

"These are great." Carter glances my way. "I'll go through them and will show you the best ones. The hardest part will be deciding which to use."

"That's a good problem to have." Grinning, I step forward and wrap Laura in a hug. "Thanks again for being a part of this article. It can't be easy sharing what you went through."

"I'm grateful I had friends who were willing to take us in." She watches her kids run around, chasing Carter on the park lawn. "I have rebuilding to do, but I believe my angels put you in front of me to remind me I have family. Family who are willing to take us in as long as needed."

"You have an interview with Maisey later today?" Following her line of sight to where Carter, Henry, and Ella are hanging on the playground, I'm honestly not sure who the bigger kid is out of the trio.

"All thanks to you two." She looks at her watch. "Kids, let's go, I've got to get ready for my meeting."

It was cute seeing the kids reluctantly say goodbye to Carter, their new playdate. Henry made sure Carter was still planning to show them around the fire station. After a pinky swear session with both kids, Laura is finally free to go.

Leaving us alone for the first time since the porch.

"So..." I clear my throat. "Thank you for jumping in to do this."

"I'm glad you asked. I'm also glad you listened."

"Are you trying to take credit for this story?"

Carter winks and hip checks me. "Well, I did say you needed to believe in yourself a little more. It's not a story about food, so I feel like I may have had some influence?"

"Maybe." These stinking butterflies are back in my stomach and holding me hostage while they do flips and tricks all over the place. "I, um, I plan on using this article to maybe help me pitch for investors."

"Really?"

I flash him a grin. "I've been working on a business plan, and I'm going to look for people who want to invest in the paper. Morris said he'd help open doors if I need, but I figure I'll start small. Use this story to stake my ground and show what I want to do with the newspaper."

"I love it, Ari." My eyes meet his and my heart begins pounding in my chest, so loud I'm worried he'll hear it. I'm caught in his hold.

Pulling away, I point to the camera in his hands. "So, I should see those pictures?"

"Definitely. The first three pictures are the money shots. I suggest using one of them for the front page. But the ones after it, I want you to see as well. In case you're interested."

"Sure." Taking the camera from his hands, I walk over to a nearby park bench and settle in. Carter slides in next to me, pressing in against my side and peering at the screen over my shoulder. I click through the first pic and see he's right. "This is great. Laura looks amazing in this shot and the kids are precious."

Flipping through the next few, I see what he means. They're all good. "You've given me a good problem, Carter. I can't pick."

He nudges me with his shoulder. "Keep clicking. There's more."

I click but I'm confused. I click a few more times, but I'm still stumped. These are photos from Charlotte—and they're pictures of me. Me talking to people at the event, me prepping the food, me drinking a coffee.

"Ha ha." I keep clicking. Only now I'm not in Charlotte. A few pictures flash by that take me back. Photos with my parents. Photos from our various birthdays, Carter's included. Pictures from high school appear. Shots of me with Reid standing at our lockers, another one of me with Mom on our way to church. Then there's one of me, with braces, grinning. Totally have food in my teeth.

"What are you doing with these?" Shaking my head, I pass the camera back to him. Certainly he's messing with me.

"I wanted you to see them, and I need you to see this." He reaches into his back pocket, pulling out his worn-out old wallet. Digging around inside it, he finds what he's after and pulls out a tiny piece of folded paper, handing it to me. I look at what it is and don't even try to stop the audible gasp escaping from my lips.

It's a photo someone had taken of me, standing between Reid and Carter at one of the Fourth of July festivals in town. Carter had taken the part of the photo with Reid in it and folded it back, so it was only him and me standing together, arms wrapped around each other.

"What is this?" My voice is but a hushed whisper.

Instead of answering, Carter reaches for my arm. It's a cool day with autumn starting to peek around the corner, and I'm wearing a light jacket over my T-shirt. He gently shoves the sleeve up my right arm, revealing my bracelet. He reaches over and fingers the lone charm dangling.

"I should have put it together." Questioning eyes meet mine. "You've kept it. All this time?"

Looking at my wrist, I realize I can't tuck it away or hide it now. I can only nod.

"Of course I have." I whisper. "You gave it to me."

"And then I told you we couldn't be together." Carter's head hangs low. "Ari, one of my biggest regrets will always be hurting you that day."

We've turned so we're facing one another, our hands intertwined. I lean in and touch my forehead to his. "We were kids. You're forgiven, okay?"

"I hurt you." His hands have come up, cupping my face as he pulls us so we're nose to nose. "I pushed you away because I didn't want to upset my best friend, but also because I never thought I'd be good enough for Ari Shannon."

Pulling back, I gawk at this man. "Are you kidding me? That's the stupidest reason I've ever heard."

"I had a lot going on at home—there's a lot I need to fill you in on—but you and your family were my safety zone. When I realized I liked pulling your hair because you gave me attention, I also knew I didn't want to do anything to ever be kicked out of the Shannons' good graces. I got to have a faux family part of the week and bonus—I got to see you, too."

While Carter bears his soul, my hands snake their way around his neck and pull him even closer into me. His arm drops down, threading around my waist. His fingertips dance on my spine. I don't want to let him go, and judging by the grip he has on me, he's feeling the same.

We sit like this for another moment. He's got his fingers in my hair now, massaging my scalp while I dance mine along his neck and shoulders, stroking the curve of his bicep. Our cheeks caressing, I drag mine across his with the end goal of placing my lips on his.

Jumping, Carter pulls away from me suddenly. I worry we're about to enter a weird moment, but he cracks up and grabs his phone out of his pocket.

"Sorry. I put it on vibrate." Holding it up, he shows me the screen.

Reid.

"Is he lining up another date?" Is my tone jealous? You bet.

Carter hits decline and sits back down, taking my hands in his. "I have no interest in anyone else, Ari. Honestly. He could set me up with a million women, but none of them are you."

"What about New York, Carter?" In case he'd forgotten, I haven't.

"What about it?"

"You have a once in a lifetime offer to run a restaurant up there. Not to be a killjoy, but I don't plan on moving, especially now that I've decided to try to get the paper."

"We can try commuting and the long distance thing...if I take the job." He looks at me. "I still don't know if I'm going to, you know."

"You want to own a restaurant. You're going to be running a food truck, getting it going for someone else, then what? You might try to open something here, but it's a year later. Maybe the guy in New York isn't interested any longer in you or he's found someone else to head up the kitchen for his Michelin five-star eatery." I shake my head. "I can't be the reason you don't take the job. Kind of like how I don't want to be the reason you and Reid get into any arguments."

"You're blowing this out of proportion." Carter stands up, combing his fingers through his hair. "We don't know what the future holds. Why should we try looking in a crystal ball for the answers? Can't you see what's happening in front of us right now?"

I sit back hard on the bench, crossing my arms and hugging my waist. The last thing I want to do is to let him go after promising myself I wouldn't, but I can't be the one who holds him back.

"Carter, I always had an idea that something was going on at your home. I saw your bruises. I know that you and your dad worked hard to repair things before he passed away. Before you freak out, Reid didn't tell me. Being a nosy little sister, I eavesdropped." I held up my arm and dangled the bracelet, flicking the football charm. "Reid gave one to Mom, and you gave me the one that was supposed to go to your mom."

Standing up, I lace his fingers through mine and put my chest against his, resting my head on his shoulder. "You've pushed down pain over the years and now you're on a trajectory to do some amazing things with your life. I want to give you a gift."

When I pull back, I see tears in his eyes as I feel the wet on my cheeks. I didn't even realize I was crying. I put my forehead back against his.

"Go and make your choices. I'm always going to be a part of your life, no matter what."

Carter screws up his face and pulls away. "You're throwing the baby out with the bath water because of a few obstacles? That's not the Ari Shannon I know and love."

Hold. The. Phone.

"Wait. Do you love me, Carter Snowden?"

I wait. He doesn't answer. "I'll ask again. Do you love me?"

Carter's mouth opens and closes. His hesitation is interesting. And annoying.

"Never mind." I grab my bag and pull out my car keys. Thank god my car is back from the shop and I don't have to beg for a ride from this guy. "This is why you should go and you do you, okay? Call the guy in New York and see what he has to say."

"Ari, wait..." Carter's protesting, but you know what? I'm not going to do this right now. To him or to myself.

I put my hand in the air. "It's fine, Carter. We can chalk up these little moments we've had to crazy hormones, the fact you're back in town, and we have history. We're both going through some life decisions and found comfort with each other. We're both a little confused."

I'm a lot confused, but eh...that's me.

"It's not that I'm confused," he murmurs. "I don't want to make the wrong decision, that's all. Does that make sense?"

"Clear as mud." Throwing my bag over my arm, I walk toward the parking lot. Turning around, I incline my chin in his direction. "Please, don't forget to send me those pictures for the article, okay?"

Do I leave now, in a royal huff because he didn't tell me he loved me? No. I'm pulling away slowly, trying to see through my tears. Of course I want to hear him say he loves me, but he can't. Makes me think he's probably right. We shouldn't even tiptoe on this line that's stretched between us and has pulled us back to one another.

But, hey...we'll always have the darkroom.

CHAPTER 10

Carter

A m I upset? A little. Not with Ari, but with myself. I had the chance to tell her I love her and, like the darkroom, I messed up. I'll never learn. I kind of deserved to be left sitting in the park alone, stewing in my feelings. Even a bird pooped on my shoulder.

When I walk into Reid's, he's playing Pac-Man. Reid's got a collection of old stand-up arcade games. Ms. Pac-Man is my favorite, but he's a sucker for the original.

"Hey." Clapping him on the back, I lean against the machine and watch as he maneuvers that little yellow maniac around the screen, gobbling ghosts along the way. There's something about him today, though. He's tense, his jaw set, and he stares at the screen in a way that tells me something's up. Even his shoulders are hiked up to his ears. "Is something wrong?"

Reid temporarily takes his eyes off the game to meet mine, before slamming them back to the screen. "I don't know. Is there?"

Huh. Why do I feel like I did something wrong? I look

around the room. Nope, I didn't leave any of my crap around, and I haven't borrowed anything or broken something that I didn't tell him about.

"If there is, I'm at a loss, dude." Crossing my arms in front of my chest, I feel the energy shift between us. I know Reid well enough to know whatever has him upset has to do with me.

We stand there in silence—me waiting for him to either win the stinking game or lose, and Reid trying not to look at me for some ridiculous reason while he puts everything he's got into winning. I have to admit, I'm upset for him when he loses his third man and the game's over. Also I'm a little nervous.

Letting go of the joystick, and without looking at me, he reaches in his pocket and pulls out his phone. "Here. The code to unlock it is my old football jersey number punched in twice."

I take the phone from his outstretched hand, punch in the code 4242 and I'm looking at a photo taken outside of Ari's place. It's from a few days ago when we got back from Charlotte at her front door, and we're very much tangled together.

This is exactly what I didn't want to happen.

"Reid, let me explain..."

Reid holds up a finger. "Do I want to hear it? Or will I get mad?"

"Honestly not sure." Walking over to the couch, I toss myself onto it. A bit harder than intended, as a spring's just dug into my butt. This guy needs a new couch. "Do I get the chance to try and tell you what that was about?"

Narrowed dark chocolate eyes meet mine as Reid leans against the game. "Okay."

Relieved, and running my fingers through my hair—nervously, because I am sweating here—I clear my throat.

"I'm falling for— No. I'm in love with your sister." Whew. It's out there.

Reid's face is unchanged. He nods his head once. "Okay."

I wasn't expecting him to encourage me, but I wasn't expecting flat-out apathy, either. I clear my throat again, thinking about my words and choosing them carefully. This is my best friend, after all.

"I think I've always been in love with her, but it wasn't until I was planning on coming back here that I got to thinking. Ari means something to me. I don't want her to be the one who got away."

I want to stand up, but I'm a little nervous he may take a swing. His hand is actually flexing. Into a fist and out. Into a fist and out. He's the son of a preacher, surely he's peaceful?

"I can see you may not be in the best place for us to talk about this right now, but I want you to know I was coming back here to tell you. I didn't like that I never told you my feelings for her and now that we're all not kids any more, I really want to see if she and I have some kind of chance."

His stony unchanging expression strikes fear into my heart. Why? Because if he doesn't like this, one way or another, I'm about to lose someone. Or both of them.

Staring at him, I watch his face for any kind of sign when I notice movement. The corner of his mouth twitches a few times. Twitches good, like he's trying to stop it from twitching and can't. I watch as it curls upward, pulling the rest of his mouth with it until his smile takes over the lower half of his face.

"Carter, I couldn't care." He bursts out laughing as he throws himself on the couch beside me, holding his stomach. "Your face! Did you really think I was going to hit you?"

"You were opening and closing your fists, of course I did! It's your little sister." My body is a confused tingle of relief, excitement, and gratitude. "Years ago, you were the one who told me to never go near her, remember?"

"That was years ago." Reid's hand slaps me on the back. "We're adulting now, right?"

I glance around the room, filled with arcade games. "Well, to a degree I guess."

Reid snorts. "When I said that stuff to you, we were kids. If you think you can make each other happy now, then do it." He sinks further into the couch, his brow furrowed. "I wondered why you didn't want to go on those dates."

"Could be because I don't want to be a guest star on the Reid and Dylan show." Seriously, I hope those two see what we're all seeing.

"Ah." He swats at me like my suggestion is a gnat. "She's Dyls. Anyway, you've got some choices to make. I think it's between New York City or my sister, right?"

Obviously he knows about the New York City offer. I'd been bleating about it the last few days, trying to decide what to do. I'd actually come up with an idea, though, and currently have my fingers crossed that it works.

"You know I'm trying to find a way to make everyone happy."

"Like a good man would." Reid throws me a mock salute. "Did you think more about the plan we came up with?"

Glancing at my watch I tap it. Three times, because...well, you know. "I have a call with Lance soon."

"What's the pitch going to be now that you've gotten all this off your chest finally?"

After rolling through my extended idea, I'm met with praise and a fist bump.

"You're a genius. Absolute genius!" Reid shakes his head laughing, before turning to me somberly. "All of this for my sister?"

"Yeah." It is and I want to tell him more, but I need some time to smooth out my own edges now and lay some plans. This time when I show up for Ari, I want to present a complete package.

"Besides the fact you love her...why? Why all of this for one person?" The look on my friend's face is genuine. Some of the conversations we've had the past few weeks have been around his own issues with relationships and how he tends to avoid them...but that's for another day. Right now, I want him to understand my "why."

"Because your sister took my heart." I chuckle, pulling out my wallet to show him the old photo of the three of us. "It took me a while to realize it and now, I never want her to give it back."

The expression crossing his face tells me everything I need to know.

"Then what are you doing here with me? Go get her."

"Yeah?"

"Yeah."

Grateful, I slap him on the back and leap to my feet. As I do, he grabs my arm.

"One thing, though. If you ever do hurt my sister, in the future...I'll find you and you won't like it. Got it?"

What am I going to say to that? Even if he is punctuating that sentence with a cheeky wink, she is his sister.

"If I ever do, and I promise you right now I won't, I'll let you tie me to the back of an ambulance and drive it full speed down Main Street. Deal?"

Reid cocks his head to the side, considering the offer. "Deal."

Laughing, I start to walk away. I need to get my notes organized before my call, but one item remains unclear.

"How did you get that picture, anyway?"

"You'll never guess." Reid's laughing. "My mom and dad. They were driving by and Mom snapped it."

"Oh, no..."

"Dude. We're all for it." Kicking out his foot, he nudges my backside with a dull kick. "Go. Get. Her."

Enough said.

CHAPTER 11
Ari

The last few days trying to not think about Carter have been beyond crazy-making. It's like when someone says "don't think about the pink elephant in the room," what are you going to do then?

Think about the pink elephant in the room. In this case, Carter is my pink elephant.

Have I spent the last few days looking at old photos, and wondering why we didn't get together years ago? Yes, I have, but I've also actively worked to not think about him. Sometimes if you shift energy, it's amazing what can happen.

I was so busy trying to keep him out of my thoughts, I got a business plan organized and managed to prepare a full presentation for potential investors to review for the Lake Lorelei News Post. Morris gladly shared his accounting details with me and even helped me forecast profit for the next few years so I can show the paper is still relevant and will make someone money if they trust me with it.

Now I need investors to pitch to, which is what I'm doing today. Sitting on my front porch going through my contacts.

Someone has to know someone I can get a meeting with, right?

Nose buried in my computer, I don't notice Reid until he's on the porch in front of me. He's like a cat, sneaking up here. Made me jump.

"You scared me."

"You should be paying more attention. I could be a robber."

"You aren't. What do you want?"

"I came by to let you know I'm mad at you." He points to where his truck is parked on the street and my stomach dips. Carter's in the passenger seat looking at me and mouthing "I'm sorry."

"Why are you mad?" I tilt my chin in the direction of his truck. "And why's he with you?"

"Give me some room, I'm coming in." My brother sits on the bench next to me, scooting me over with his hip. He throws his arm around my neck, pulling me close. "Confession time. That guy in the truck, he told me everything."

My face burns when Reid shows me the picture that my parents took. I fly off the seat, horrified.

"So. You know." I stare at my feet, keeping my back to the truck where Carter sits, wanting the porch to swallow me. Why isn't Carter out here with me taking it? Of course, Reid's already had a go at him, which is why they're here. My turn for a "come to Jesus" moment.

"Yeah, I know, alright." Reid snorts, standing up. "Like I told that one"—he points to the truck—"if you two don't figure it out once and for all, I'll stop speaking to both of you."

"Reid, I...wait. You're okay with it?"

"Yeah, dummy." He shakes his head. "What am I, an ogre who doesn't want you to be happy? No. I'd be mad if you two didn't try after fighting your feelings all this time. I'm not going to get in your way."

He holds his hand up, waving for Carter to join us. I turn around and watch as he gets out of the truck and makes his way over to the porch, coming to a stop at the bottom of the steps.

He teases me with one of his half-smiles. "Hi."

"Hi. You told him."

"Yep."

We stand there, awkwardly. Me? I'm fidgeting, looking back and forth at Carter and Reid. Carter's bright green eyes bounce between Reid's and mine, and Reid, looking at us both and shaking his head.

"I know when I'm a third wheel." He leans over and hugs me, then slaps Carter on the back as he walks down the steps, heading to his truck. "I'm going to leave you two alone. You've got some things to figure out."

Shocked, I watch him fire up the ignition and take off up my street in that bright red truck of his. He waves out the window as he disappears from my vision. Leaving us alone.

Biting my lower lip, I drag my eyes to meet Carter's. They simmer, waves of seduction rising up to greet me. "Hi again."

"Hey." Carter puts a foot tentatively on the bottom step. "Mind if I come up?"

Nodding, I point to the empty bench. "Of course not."

We sit, his hands on his knees. Seeing them tremble, I reach out and cover them with mine. "That was unexpected."

Flashing that charming smirk of his, he turns in his seat to face me. His fingertips caress the skin of my forearms, dancing their way along the path from my wrist up to my shoulder. His touch sends thousands of tiny electrical currents racing through my body causing a shiver to race up and down my spine.

"It threw me, too." He takes a deep breath. "I'll tell you

what happened with Reid, but first I need to talk to you about New York."

My stomach clenches. "What did you decide?"

"I spoke with Lance and pitched him a new idea. I hope you don't mind what I did."

Staying quiet, I wait for him to go on.

"I want the opportunity to open a restaurant, but when I started to look at properties in the area here, I realized I may not be able to do it on my own. I've got to admit, it was really good timing for Lance to want me to come be his chef. I saw my chance at opening a restaurant, doing what I want."

Telling my stomach to calm down isn't working right now. I think he senses my worry because Carter pulls me in close, wrapping his arms around me. Curled against his chest, I lay my head on it listening to his heart beat as he speaks. If he's about to tell me what I think he is, at least I'm in the cuddle zone of happiness.

"I spoke to Lance and told him my ideas, Ari. What I want to do when I open my own restaurant. In fact, we spoke at length the other day about what it will look like when Lance backs my idea."

Swallowing, I pull back some so I can look at this man. Our eyes find one another, and I lower my forehead to gently touch his. "Lance would be a fool to not invest in you. You're good at what you do, and as sad as I'll be that you'll be there, I can't blame you for taking the opportunity."

"That's the thing, Ari." Carter pulls away and grabs me by the shoulders. "I'm not going to New York, New York is coming to Lake Lorelei."

Surely I've heard him wrong. "Come again?"

"Lance is on his way down today for a visit. He's coming in to look at a space here in town with me." He stands up, holding out his arms. "He's going to back me here in Lake Lorelei."

Shock, happiness, comfort, confusion...they all hit my system at once but are overridden by excitement. I leap to my feet, throwing my arms around his neck and wrapping my legs around his waist.

"Are you kidding me?" Laughing, he spins in a circle, still holding me up propped on his frontside. Slowing to a stop, he places me back on my feet. "I feel like we need to celebrate."

Buzzing, I start to turn away, but Carter grabs my wrist and spins me around. "There's more. You're going to want to sit down for this one, sunshine."

Hugging my waist, I stare him down. "This is a good news-only zone at the moment, so unless you're telling me you won the lottery and I get to borrow the money to buy the paper, I don't wanna hear it."

"It's not that I won the lottery. We won it, Ari."

Oh, that grin. It's back and it's sexy. Chewing on his lower lip, he reaches out and puts a hand on each hip, pulling me close. Toe to toe, chest to chest, nose to nose. His skin brushes mine as he runs his fingers up the back of my spine.

"What do you mean?"

"I told Lance about the paper closing. How you were looking for someone to potentially invest in it. He's very excited to meet you and see your business plan, if it's ready?"

"What?" Stunned, I take a step back. "No."

"Yes. The space we're looking at for the restaurant is on the first floor of the building that the newspaper is in. When I explained to him it would all be in one building he was ready to make an offer immediately. Turns out our little area here at the lake is getting quite a good reputation for being a safe place to raise your family as well as a great spot for summer tourism."

I can't even handle all of this news. My knees knock together as I slowly lower myself back to the bench, but strong masculine arms are pulling me back up. Pressing me into his chest.

"So you'll be able to present your business plan to Lance later this week?"

Nodding my head, I'm surprised when my eyes begin watering. Wet hits my cheeks, and Carter's hand comes up, wiping away my tears.

"Hey," he whispers, kissing my forehead. "It's good news, right? I really hope it is because if you only knew what I went through to get us here."

"No. I mean, yes! It's great news." Planting a hand on either side of his face, I hold it still so I can look at him. Not just in a glance, but fully taking in his features and surface bits. I want to look into the depths of those flashing green eyes and see his soul. Placing my hand on his chest, I feel the rhythm of his heart speeding up as my eyes are pulled to his lips.

Dragging his hand up the side of my body, causing dips and twists to my insides like nobody's business, it comes to a rest on my cheek. His calloused thumb ever so gently circles my lips. I clutch his T-shirt, pulling him closer to me so our mouths are merely inches away from each other.

"It's the best news ever," I whisper as I reach up, wrapping my other arm around his neck and pulling his mouth to mine. Soft and gentle, his hands push my hair away from my face and his fingers tangle in my hair.

I could stay right here forever.

He kisses me and kisses me some more, until my body's melted like chocolate into his and my mind is thick with fog.

Pulling away, I lay my head on his shoulder. "You know, Maisey's going to take credit for this."

Carter erupts into laughter. "Oh, you bet she will. Who would've thought a food truck with giant donuts on top would bring us together?"

"I can hear it now. 'I've got an idea, you guys. I'm calling it

Donuts and Date Night.'" Am I giggling ridiculously? You bet I am. "It took The Sweet Spot to help us find ours, Carter."

"Better late than never." Tilting his head, Carter places his lips to my ear, his voice low. "I love you, Ari Shannon."

"I love you, too, Carter Snowden." Closing my eyes, I rest my cheek against his. Never have I felt so safe, so right.

It's true what they say. Love is like a puzzle: you find your other half and it fits. It just takes time for some of us to get there. After all, we don't find love.

It always finds us.

CHAPTER 12

Carter

"Are you sure she's going to like it?"

"I really hope so." I chuck a pillow at my alleged best buddy. It's a bittersweet day for us guys, with Reid helping me pack my things to move in with Ari.

"I still can't believe she has no idea what you're up to." He chuckles, tossing a few of my books in a box. "The fact my parents were so agreeable should have been a clue."

My lips twitch, fighting a smile. It has been a busy month for both Ari and myself. Lance had come from New York and fallen in love with the News Post building, almost as much as I love Ari. He was already excited about the restaurant possibility, but when he met Ari and heard her ideas, he was over the moon. The paperwork was signed and hands were shaken on that inaugural trip.

"Your parents have been an incredible support, man." Pat and Mike had been checking in on both of us as Ari got the newspaper going, settling into her new role as editor-in-chief with ease. On nights when she worked late, if I wasn't showing up with dinner for her, Ari's parents were dropping off a casserole for the both of us.

Mike also made his presence known, coming in between writing his weekly sermons to see the work being done on the restaurant. He'd become a second assistant to me, helping oversee the construction workers when I needed to slip out to handle The Sweet Spot—being someone who likes to bite off more than he can chew sometimes, I decided to go in with Maisey and co-own the food truck operation with her. Life has been a full on team effort, and we're winning.

"Well, they love you and always have. I can only hope that when I finally meet 'the one' she's as well received as the two of you have been."

Grinning, I grab some of my dishes and pack them away. The windows are open letting in a fresh breeze, but the chill of the November evening is beginning to snake its way in. Throwing a hoodie over my head, I push my arms through and point to the clock.

"It's almost go-time. Is Maisey still coming?"

"Yep. Said Laura would have The Sweet Spot outside to pick you up promptly at six."

"Awesome." Crossing my arms in front of me, I look at my friend and indicate to his row of arcade games. "It's been a blast having game night every night. Think about my offer, and Lance's. You can bring those games into the restaurant. We've got room and they'll totally fit the vibe."

"Oh, you know I am," he chortles. "I'll let you know."

His eyes dart past me. Following his gaze out the front window, I see a familiar sight parked in the driveway. Two giant donuts, like a beacon for my heart.

"My chariot awaits." Turning, I put my hand out to shake Reid's. He looks at my hand, his face twisting until he cracks up. "What are you doing? Come here."

He grabs me, pulling me in for a giant hug before pushing me away when Laura honks the horn. "Good luck."

Touching the small box in my pocket, I cross my fingers. This is one night where I hope I don't need luck on my side.

* * *

"I thought you were going to my place and dropping boxes off?"

My beautiful woman stands in front of me, a hot mess. A hot mess on deadline at her paper. Hot is the key word because I don't think she could look any sexier. Her blonde hair is pulled away from her face, showing off that luscious neck of hers. I've become obsessed with trailing kisses from her shoulder to her ear, thank you very much. Thankfully, she doesn't mind.

"Change of plans." Jerking my thumb over my shoulder, I tug on her wrist gently with my free hand. Behind her, the office is busy with her staff working hard to make their tight deadline. "I know you're slammed, but do you have a second to see something?"

She narrows her eyes, but I know she's not irritated. It's playful, like us. Like every day has been since we slammed back into each other's lives. Blissful, yes. Nights staying up late talking about our hopes, wants, fears, and dreams? You bet. I've loved every sleepless minute of it. If I wasn't positive she was the one before—which I was, so don't get me wrong—I am one hundred percent cemented in the faith of us now.

"You know, I get weird if there's too much change." She slips her hand in mine. "But, I trust you. Lead me."

We make our way downstairs and outside the building where The Sweet Spot sits parked against the curb. The window is open and the smells of Maisey's best donuts and baked goods assaults our senses. Brewed coffee dances in the air, and I watch as Ari's nose follows it, like a puppy smelling a treat on the counter.

"Oh, you're the best. You brought us treats?"

"Kind of."

We walk up to the counter where two fresh brewed cups of coffee wait.

"Pumpkin pecan latte?" Reaching out, Ari swipes a cup, takes a sip, and smiles. "You're the best. This is worth everything to me right now."

"But wait, there's more." I grab a pink pastry box sitting on the stainless steel ledge. "I've made some special donuts for you."

Ari grabs the box from my hands, but I snatch it back. "Hang on. Let's sit down and eat. We're not animals."

Laughing, she skips over to the stoop in front of the News Post building and plops down, holding her hand out. "Gimme some sugar, sugar."

It's now or never.

"Before I do, I want to tell you I love you."

"I. Love. You. Now, hand me that." She leans over and tries to open the lid, but I snap at her hand with the lid, like Richard Gere did to Julia Roberts in Pretty Woman—it's my favorite romantic comedy. Don't judge me, I'm in touch with my masculine side, but I know what makes her happy, too. "No need to get physical. I'm really excited there's a pink glazed one in there, that's all."

I inhale deeply. It's time.

"You know I've loved you for a long time, Ari Shannon."

"Yes, but I love donuts, too. Am I going to get to eat one?"

"Listen." Leaning over, I plant a kiss on her lips to get her to stop talking. "It wasn't until I came back that I understood what it means to love someone so much it aches inside. To be the keeper of secrets with someone else in this world is so special, and I'm going to tell you every day as long as I can how grateful and lucky I am."

"You know I love you, too." She cocks her head to one side, reaching out to stroke my cheek. "Where is all of this coming from? You're not having second thoughts about moving in together, are you?"

Placing the pink box in her hands, I drop down on one knee. Ari's eyes widen and her jaw goes slack. Worried she's going to drop her coffee, I reach out and take it from her hand and place it on the step beside her.

"I want to show you something, but I have a question, too."

Peeling the lid of the box open, I present the special package to her. Maisey had helped, of course, and made several flavors of donuts, but it's the diamond ring placed on top of her favorite pink glazed donut which catches her eye.

"Carter." Gasping, her eyes rocket to meet mine.

"I think it's time I put a ring on it." Taking the ring from its sugary perch, I hold it out to her. "Will you marry me?"

She doesn't answer right away, her lips instead finding mine. Covering my mouth, she tells me her answer as her arms thread their way around my neck, pulling me in. But of course I have to hear it.

Pulling back, I place my forehead on hers. It's become our thing. I like it because it's like we're frozen and breathing one another in...and I can kiss her if I want.

"So it's a yes?" I whisper.

Deep, sweet brown eyes full of promise, love, and unchartered waters meet mine. "I do. I will. I can, and yes, I'll marry you, Carter Snowden, and love all of you, every insane inch— even if it comes with weekly dates with my brother—for today, for tomorrow, and for always."

Epilogue

ARI

"Is it time to throw the bouquet yet?"

Dylan stands in front me, one hand planted resolutely on her hip. "You know, the guys from the firehouse said they'd pay me twenty bucks each if I catch it."

"They did what?" Sighing, I glance over at Reid and shake my fist in the air. Only my brother could make my wedding day a competitive sporting occasion.

Hold on a second. I need to savor this moment. It's *my* wedding day––and it's been perfect. From the moment I woke up, I have been on cloud nine and have floated from location to location with only my bridesmaids, and my heart, to guide me.

There was the moment I walked down the aisle when Carter turned around and we locked eyes. It has to be my all time favorite snapshot from the day and it's a memory I'll hold onto for the ages. In that brief second, I felt everything for him. My stomach dipped with excitement as I caught my breath, a heady rush causing me to hold my father's arm tighter.

After the wedding, which was at my father's church of

course, Carter insisted we all walk as a group down Main Street to the reception. He threw open the doors of the church to lead us out, and as he did the Lake Lorelei marching band started playing. This talented group surrounded us with music all the way to the Red Bird...a gift courtesy of his fellow fire-fighters.

Now, standing inside the Red Bird, I'm looking across the cafe and eyeing up a group of guys I know well, all of them firefighters, huddling in the corner. "When you say 'the guys', how many have made this bet?"

Dylan's face scrunches as she does a quick calculation. "I could win $160."

"Okay...tell you what. Let's get two more on board, bring it to an even $200 bet, split it with me and I'll make sure you get the bouquet."

"Deal."

Laughing, I watch Dylan trot away to stir the pot--I mean, make us some money--when something bumps my hand. Moments later, I feel something soft sliding across my skin as Carter threads his fingers through mine and squeezes my hand. Leaning over, he plants a soft kiss on my cheek.

"Hello Mrs. Snowden. Having a good day?"

I pull my attention away from the dance floor and plant it firmly on my man. "Well, Mr. Snowden, I've had a fabulous day. Thank you for asking."

Man, I'm one lucky lady. Let's be honest; he's a VERY lucky man... but ladies, my husband cooks. And guess what else he insists on doing? The grocery shopping. The moment he asked me to marry him, do you really think I was going to say no based on those two items of info alone?

Pulling me close, Carter nuzzles the nape of my neck. "What were you and Dylan over here talking about?"

"Just talking. Nothing you need to worry about."

"I feel like there's more to it, especially when I look across the room and see her father giving cash to Reid." Carter leans in closer to me, sniffing the air. "Something stinks to me."

"Considering how many firefighters we have gathered in this room, you could be smelling smoke or some other kind of fumes?"

"Ha. Now, Dylan's over there sitting on your brother's lap and it looks like she's trying to talk him into something. Are you going to tell me it has nothing to do with whatever the two of you were over here discussing?"

"A lady likes to keep her secrets." I slowly lift one shoulder and let it drop, as if shrugging off his question. The distraction does its job––laughing, Carter tugs on my hand, leading me out to the dance floor and pulls me close in his arms. Resting my head on his chest, I finally let out a sigh of relief.

"That was an enormous sigh," he murmurs in my ear, his lips brushing against my earlobe with a featherlight touch.

"It's been a big day and as much fun as I'm having, I can't wait to get on that plane for the Caribbean."

"Me, too." Carter's hands are already holding me close, but now he places one hand on each hip, pulling me in closer against his body as he trails a few discreet kisses from my earlobe to my shoulder. "I have more surprises for you once we're there."

"I can't wait to get them." Giggling, I swat him playfully. "But right now, I have to sort out a bouquet toss."

"Why is this bouquet toss such a big deal today? Dub was trying to talk Jack into betting on Dylan that she'd catch it, but Jack mentioned putting his money on Maisey... did I miss the memo?"

"No, it seems we're surrounded by people who love to make up games and reasons to compete, even at a wedding." Cutting my eyes across the room, I witness the moment Reid palms a twenty-dollar bill into Dylan's waiting hand. Catching her eye after the transaction is complete, we give each other the thumbs up. "But we're also surrounded by people who love winning. All I can say is bet on Dylan."

At that moment, something––or someone, rather––slams into our right side. It's like we're the Titanic and we just nailed an iceberg. "Did I hear you right, Ari Shannon Snowden? Did you tell your husband to bet on Dylan for the bouquet toss?"

Maisey is suddenly beside us, moving slowly back and forth to the music with Jack. Funny thing is, they look really cute together.

"Maybe I did," I call out over my shoulder while Carter spins me around in a circle on the dance floor. "Why are you in a betting mood?"

"No." Maisey hisses, nudging Jack to move closer to where we're dancing. "But I want to win some money. Jack, Laura, and some of the team from the kitchen bet me I won't be able to catch the bouquet. If I do, I get $200."

I love where this is going and bless his dear heart; it seems my dear husband does too.

Carter's eyes find mine, dancing with laughter. Not just dancing... they are boogying down. "So, let me get this straight, Maisey. If you catch the bouquet, you'll get $200 total?"

Maisey bobs her head up and down enthusiastically. "Not that I care about the money. I want to win, you know?"

Oh, I know. This woman can compete with a capital C. I invited her to my bachelorette game night, and it was carnage. I never knew that running charades could turn into an all out war. When Maisey decides she's going to win, she. Is. Going. To. Win.

"Roger that." Carter's lopsided grin is back, and it makes my heart skip a beat. "I guess we may need to help you out here, right, sweetie?"

"Right." I wink slyly at Carter as he spins me right around

to face Maisey and Jack. "Split that money with me and I'll help you out, Maisey."

Reaching over Jack's broad shoulders, Maisey holds her hand out to grasp mine. "Deal."

"Satisfied?" Jack chuckles to his dance partner, laughing as he turns her in a circle and begins moving them toward the other side of the dance floor. "We'll leave you two alone to dance in peace now."

Carter chuckles and looks at me, his twinkling green eyes meeting mine. "Seems everyone is trying to cash in on our wedding."

"We've got two horses in this race, it would seem." I close my eyes and chew on my laughter for a few seconds. Carter's arms squeezing me around my middle bring me back to the present.

"You don't feel bad you just pitted them against each other?"

Tilting my head to one side, I think about the question for a hot minute before answering. "Well, either way, we stand to get $100 out of it. It'll teach them a lesson. Don't go to a wedding and start placing bets."

"I guess I should let you know that the guys at the station had a bet on whether we'd have the garter toss," Carter says while laughing.

"Of course I knew." Craning my neck to the side, I find a better angle to take in those gorgeous eyes of his. I forget how tall he is sometimes until I'm pressed right up against his rock hard body. "Reid told me all about it... after I told him we weren't doing it because I think it's gross. I didn't want someone I'm not married to taking a garter off my leg in front of a room full of people––some of whom have known me since I was in my diapers."

"But you'll pit two of your friends against each other for a bouquet toss?"

"Shhh. It's about the money, Carter." I pull him close to me and start swaying to the music again. "And the flowers. I mean, who doesn't want a gorgeous bouquet of fresh flowers to take home? Let 'em work for it."

Laughing, Carter clutches me at the waist even tighter right as the sound system comes alive around us.

"Testing, testing... can everyone hear me?"

Glancing across the room, I find my brother has taken control of the microphone. We could be in trouble.

"Hey everybody. If we haven't met, I'm Reid and I'm the brother of the bride. I'm also the best man because that guy," he shouts, pointing with full on dramatic flair to Carter, "has been my best friend since we were kids. Like little boys in kindergarten, that kind of little. Now, judging by the expression of fear on my sister's face, I can tell she doesn't want me to stay up here for too long..."

"Good observation," I call out, catching my mother's eye. "Can you get that thing from him, Mom?"

As my mother shrugs, throwing her hands in the air like she isn't able to help me out––come on, we all know that sons listen to their mothers!––Reid waves a hand in the air and continues.

"Shush, Ari. It's my day to be nice to my little sister." He stops, looking down at his feet before pulling his head up to address the room and when he does, something is different. I can tell he's nervous. Even from my vantage point in the middle of the dance floor, I spy a small bead of sweat sliding ever so slowly down the side of his face. Between the heat outside and all the people packed into the Red Bird today, thank goodness the ceiling fans are on and keeping the air flowing, otherwise my big brother would be a puddle of water.

"Ari, I'm speaking on behalf of the whole family when I say that we're so proud of you. You've reached such great heights, as mom says, and you have a drive and a determination which has powered you the whole way. As your big bro, I would like to think you got some of that from me, but there's no way. You are a spitfire of energy, a woman who sees what she wants and makes it happen, and you do all of this with an ease that makes people like me wonder how you keep it all together."

Reid then angles his body, focusing on Carter. "And you, you call yourself my best friend? It took me years to get you to admit what we all knew... that you loved my sister. I am so glad you figured it out and finally owned up to it, because there's no one else I would rather have as my brother-in-law than someone I already consider a true brother."

I can feel something wet on my cheek at the same time I hear Carter's breath hitch beside me. My hand flies up to brush away the tear that has snuck its way out of my eye and makes its way down the side of my face. Growing up a little sister, you get used to being teased and, for lack of a better term, tortured by your older siblings. But it's the relationships that come out of those learning years, the childhood bonding. Those are the ones that are the most important. They build our foundation for who we become, both alone and as brother and sister. And at this moment, I'm so glad I've got Reid as my big brother. I know he'll always have my back just as fiercely as I will always have his.

At some point, someone must have shoved a couple of champagne flutes into our hands. Carter and I both raise our glasses and tilt our libations toward the front of the room, where Reid stands to thank him.

And, just like that... the moment is over and we're back to the Reid show.

"Now, on to the important part of the day. Time to toss that bridal bouquet! Let's get some ladies out on the dance floor!"

I feel a sudden sting as a hand smacks my bottom. Turning around, I catch Maisey standing with a hand on her hip and a huge grin on her face. She points to a spot right in the very middle of the dance floor that coincidentally, is next to Dylan.

"I'll stand there, okay?"

"You bet," I nod, watching her walk away. Making sure Maisey can't see me, I flag Dylan, holding up a hand and showing her to stay put where she is while I get into position.

For the love of all things sugar, I don't want to choose who is going to catch this bouquet. I'm going to let the two of them battle it out the old-fashioned way. Reid has pulled me to the front of the room and Mom hands me my bouquet. It's the most perfect collection of my favorite flowers, all bunched up together. Roses, lilies, and tulips are in shades of red and pink which all complement one another and the other colors used to decorate in the cafe.

On the dance floor in front of me, the fabulous women of Lake Lorelei are gathering. Those wearing heels understand the nature of this moment and kick their shoes off to the side. And some are in their Sunday finest and are taking a moment to make sure shirts are tucked in and jewelry is secured. No one needs their clothes ripped or any other kind of fashion emergency to happen in front of the whole town.

"Last call," Reid sings out into the mic. "Come on out and get on the dance floor. Married, single. It's an all-inclusive bouquet toss because my sister said so."

A cheer rings out from the crowd, making me giggle. Being a former single lady, I never appreciated being called out at a wedding for being one, thus my insistence on everyone taking part--no matter who they are.

As the moment arrives, I scan the crowd one last time. Maisey holds out her hands and bobs her head while next to her. Dylan winks my way and rubs her fingertips together, giving me the universal 'cash' sign. Next thing I know, Carter's hands are on my shoulders and he spins me around to face him as Reid begins the countdown.

The smile on Carter's face is so big it's like it's eating his head. God, I love this man. "Ready?"

I nod my head. "Yep."

"Here we go!" Reid points to the back of the room, where Dub and Jack begin a drumroll on their table. "Five. Four. Three. Two....ONE!"

Leaning back and closing my eyes, I release the bouquet. In my mind's eye, it's going to sail through the air and land in front of Dylan and Maisey, allowing one of them the time to snatch it from the other's grasp and hopefully without too much drama.

But things never go as planned, do they?

As the bouquet leaves my grasp, and before I open my eyes, I hear gasps of surprise and someone shouts "turn the fan off!" in the distance. Snapping my eyes open, I turn around in time to witness my beautiful bouquet connecting with a ceiling fan turned up to high speed.

Honestly, it is a beautiful and unique sight for a brief spell. It's like a sudden rainfall has hit us, only instead of water droplets, its pieces of lilies, tulips, and roses we're being showered with. In direct contradiction to the sight of the flower petals being strewn about, the sound of the bouquet as it slams into the fan is horrendous. The intense buzzing sound it makes, like a weed eater would, jolts most of the partygoers into a duck-cover situation, which thankfully protects anyone from having a stray stem fly through the air and put an eye out.

Thankfully, we have no injuries. As the commotion dies down, I look around for Maisey and Dylan, wondering what's happened to them in all of this ruckus. I know they're going to be disappointed to not win any money now, all thanks to my poor tossing skills.

Turns out, I needn't have worried.

When my eyes come across the two ladies, both Dylan and Maisey are triumphantly holding parts of the now-shredded bouquet in their hands.

My jaw goes slack as Carter presses his lips to my ear. "By my calculation, I think we've made $200 today since both ladies caught the bouquet?"

Laughing, I throw my arms around his neck and grin. Looking into those eyes of his, I know I'm right where I'm supposed to be––and I'm ready for our forever to start now. Leaning in, I softly drag my lips across his, only daring to brush them ever so slowly. Teasing and real. For love and for laughter. For now and for tomorrow.

Nuzzling his face in my hair, Carter wraps his arms around me. "I'm so lucky you said yes."

"I'm so lucky you asked." Kissing his forehead, I pull back and cup his face with my hands. "To our always."

Soft lips come down on mine, pulling away only to whisper back. "May it be forever."

Thank you!

Thank you so much for reading The Sweet Spot!

This book is part of the Love in Lake Lorelei Series and I'd love to introduce you to Freya and Wyatt in Sweet Summer Nights - available in Kindle Unlimited, eBook & paperback.

Want to stay up to date with my new releases, get in on bonus giveaways, and have a free book delivered to your email each week?
Sign up for my newsletter! Go to:
www.annekemp.com

Acknowledgments

There are always so many people to thank in my village and with each book, the village gets bigger!

The first shout out is to my poor husband who gets to listen to me talk about these books always BUT who also makes me dinner every night so I don't have to worry about it. When I'm writing, I can stay in my cave and he makes sure we're still fed!

Authors seem to always gather the COOLEST people around them, well..that's my experience! During the process of getting The Sweet Spot out there, I called on my community on BookTok and Bookstagram to help, and y'all did not disappoint! Thank you for your constant support, I am so beyond grateful for you.

To my Beta readers, ARC team, and Street Team: I am SO LUCKY to have found you! One day I hope I get to stand in a room with you all to give you my thanks in person.

To the Writer Frenz (you know who you are) THANK YOU for holding my hand when I need it and know mine is here for you in return... always.

Lastly, to Sabrina, welcome and thank you for being an angel!

Anne x

Also by Anne Kemp

Love in Lake Lorelei Series

These Sweet RomComs are sizzling with chemistry, set in North Carolina, and are bringing you all the feels!

Get to know the locals and, most importantly, the

Lake Lorelei Fire Department!

Sweet Summer Nights (Book 1)

Freya and Wyatt's story

The Sweet Spot (Book 2)

Ari and Carter's story

When Sparks Fly (Book 3)

Maisey and Jack's story: coming Christmas '22

The Abby George Series

The Abby George books are closed-door, Chick lit comedies with a lil' sass, a touch of sarcasm, and some language (especially from the salty captain!)... but are guaranteed to have you laughing out loud as you fall in love!

Rum Punch Regrets

Gotta Go To Come Back

Sugar City Secrets

Caribbean Romance Novellas

Part of the Abby George world but can be read as stand

alones. These books are sweet and clean closed door romantic comedies.

The Reality of Romance

Second Chance for Christmas

About the Author

Anne Kemp is an author of romantic comedies, sweet
contemporary romance, and chick lit.
She loves reading (and does it ridiculously fast, too!), gluten-
free baking
(because everyone needs a hobby that makes them crazy), and
finding time to binge-watch her favorite shows. She grew up in
Maryland but made Los Angeles her home until she
encountered her own real-life meet-cute at a friend's wedding
where she ended up married to one of the groomsmen.
For real.

Anne now lives on the Kapiti Coast in New Zealand, and even
though she was married at Mt. Doom, no...she doesn't have a
Hobbit. However, she and her husband do have a terrier
named George Clooney and a rescue pup named Charlie.
When she's not writing, she's usually with them taking a long
walk on the river by their home.

You can find Anne on her website www.annekemp.com or
find her on social media.
She's on TikTok andInstagram as @annekempauthor
and on Facebook and Twitter @missannekemp.

Made in the USA
Monee, IL
12 August 2022